Creatures of the Lord

By

Craig Leibfreid

Chapter 1: Behavioral Health

Todd sat in in his chair in the group counseling room at Buena Vista behavioral health center in Santa Barbara California, his shaved head and neck tattoo glaring the meek female counselor in the face as she explained the importance of sleep and diet. There were about ten people in the 40 X 40 room with big windows and wooden floors. The television behind the counselor was turned off. Tara was the professional's name. The mental health patients were all suffering from various ailments. Anxiety, depression, bipolar disorder, schizophrenia, PTSD. Todd had an offensive exterior. His schizoaffective disorder made him a little hard to handle, a combination of schizophrenia and bipolar-mania. Hallucinations, grandeur, delusions, hyperactivity, but there were ways of beating his demons. The medication was working, and he took Tara's words for truth, but there was more to his health than modern medicine. Tara was speaking the ideology of decades of psychological research.

Eric was a tall thin man, one of the more easy-going patients out of the fifteen delinquents who sat before the counselor. There were drunks, drug users, and psychotics. All present, but not all open to the advice and treatment they would be billed for. It's hard to buy into someone else's principles of reason, and that includes the clinically insane. Digesting the standards of mental health and emotional stability can be appalling. When another tells you that you aren't living the right way or acting the right way because your brain is malfunctioning, it's insulting. Some of the patients were able to accept the criticism. Most were not. Todd and Eric among the minority open to the suggestions of the mental health professionals. Eric was still coming down off the ten hits of LSD he was talked into taking a few weeks prior. His hallucinations were vivid. The fear and inner tension were wild. It was too much. The drug caused the mind to twist and scream for mercy. Then, in only moments, it reeled in delight. The rollercoaster of emotions and overload of sensory perception takes the mind far beyond what a person is meant to handle. Eric took far too much acid. The trip was intense, and he never really came down. He hoped a trip to the hospital would bring him back to sanity. His friends dropped him off at the hospital, and eventually, Eric ended up at Buena Vista. As the weeks passed, the hallucinations declined, but he was vacant. He felt no passion. Hope was a complete mystery.

Tara refrained from talking about anything spiritual or religious. She stuck to what could be explained in textbooks and medical journals. Todd on the other hand was open about his faith, and kept it close to his heart. He wasn't always a religious man. He battled mental illness most of his adult life, untreated both medically and spiritually until he landed in prison. Mental instability sent him on crime sprees in his twenty's. Now at the age of 35, older and wiser, he could tell when he needed help. He didn't want to end up as a convict doing hard time all of his life. He vaguely listened as Tara went on in the group session.

"Extreme lack of sleep can cause disruption to the body's production of serotonin which leads to..." Tara squeaked out.

Todd was losing interest. Freedom was on his mind. He was due to be released the next day just after breakfast. The future was a mystery for him. He was stable. He came in with uncontrollable stamina and energy. Not so much of the physical type, but mentally and vocally. He was talking uncontrollably, and his mind was racing. It was something beyond mere anxiety or paranoia. He was manic. The confines of Buena Vista and the adjustments to his medication quelled the feelings of bewilderment running ramped through his soul. Group ended. The patients broke apart and waited to be called to lunch. Todd walked out to the hall where Eric was standing by one of the windows. Eric had so many questions: What to ask of life, and how to get whatever that might be? He lost most of his ability to socialize. He felt soulless. He felt like all passion was gone. As he turned to his left, he was surprised to see Todd standing next to him.

"A free man once more come tomorrow!" Todd expressed to Eric with genuine happiness in his voice.

"Yeah, I'm getting released tomorrow too." Eric sounded unsure of himself.

"Still not back yet?"

Todd knew about Eric's acid trip. The hallucinations. The hopelessness and helplessness. It was a lot like the schizophrenia symptoms Todd had to deal with.

"Man, you need to have a little more faith in yourself."

"Hah, faith how can a man believe in anything, even himself. The heart lies. The head fears."

"That acid really robbed you of your soul."

"Soul? I don't believe in that stuff. No proof."

"I thought the Jesus-people movement came from the acid culture? You know, when the ancient Greeks sent a man off into the afterlife, they never asked about a man's soul, they only asked if he had passion. Soul, passion, I don't see much difference."

Todd's words provoked something in Eric. They weren't strong enough to inspire passion for anything in Eric, but it made faith in a higher power, something supernatural, more tangible. He tasted sounds and heard colors. What's not to say there's a real God someone could believe in and draw strength from. Todd had seen a lot of hell. He shared a lot of wisdom with lanky, hipster Eric. They were kind of friends. Eric heard Todd out, but wasn't always listening. He lost his capacity for empathy towards things spiritual. He felt so hollow that all of that seemed to be a myth, at least to him. Before overdosing, the twenty-two-year-old spent his days sipping coffee in southern-California coffee-shops with his shaggy black hair, khaki shorts, and designer sunglasses. He thought soul was something that could be bought just like a Les Paul guitar or his Black Keys vinyls. He never did acid before taking that ten-strip, but that seemed to rob him of the soul he thought he had. The superficial passions that he chased in life now seemed worthless, no matter how visceral or primal they may have once felt.

"You know, I always felt like people were after me, which should have steered me away from crime, but it only made me a better fugitive. When I got diagnosed with schizoaffective disorder, the meds helped but what really brought me comfort was faith in Christ, a relationship with God."

Sassy Eric would have asked if that should comfort him, but after hitting rock bottom, Eric put a little more thought into Todd's words.

"Lunch!" a voice yelled from down the hall.

Chapter 2: Wine, Jesus!

It was 4:10 PM in Santa Barbara, early June. The #7 bus arrived at stop 296 on Cliff St. Todd was leaning against a street post, waiting for Eric. The doors opened, and out shuffled a few people in to the balmy air and brilliant sun. Eric had a paper bag full of clothes in his hands, and a look in his eyes that said he was running on fumes. He squinted at the sun, and sighed at the beautiful weather. Todd and his wisdom were the only thing that kept him moving forward.

"Come on, Eric."

The stocky bald man with the neck tattoo tried to comfort the vacant hipster. Todd had a lot of love in his heart. He could see the pain in Eric's eyes and he wanted to make a difference. Provide him a little faith, hope, and happiness. It was a Monday afternoon, and both men were scheduled for outpatient therapy beginning next week, but the freedom of the real-world was upon them. They wanted to enjoy the newness of it all. That would be a little tough for Eric in the midst of his depression, but Todd pushed him on as they walked the streets of Santa Barbara.

"Let's go somewhere that I can get a pack of smokes."

Todd chuckled.

"You're in an American city," he laughed. "It's called a convenience store."

Eric Just shook his head.

"Did you ever think about giving those things up? They can't help. Just make you sick eventually."

"You're gonna tell me to sacrifice the simplest form of comfort I can get?"

"There's more comfort in faith, man."

"What is it with you and faith?"

"Once you find it, its stronger than anything."

Eric and Todd walked side by side. Eric held his head low with sunglasses hiding his eyes, and Todd gazed out over the streets and buildings, watching the people rush home from work in the afternoon. The bright sun and warm ocean breeze brought no pleasure to Eric. He just wandered in the abyss of his mind, hoping for that cigarette. Eventually they found a convenience store. Todd and Eric walked in, and in front of them was a tall man with long dark hair wearing a white cotton robe. He was buying a bottle of wine. Todd was munching something over in his mind. Eric just thought, "Look at this weirdo." The man bought his wine, and slowly walked to the door in his rope sandals. Eric bought his Camel lights, and the three of them headed back to the street. Eric hit the sidewalk and pulled a smoke from the pack. He put it between in his lips, and as he reached for the lighter in his pocket, the man in the white robe said,

"Why are you doing that, Eric?"

Eric looked a bit confused about how this stranger knew his name.

"Meek hope, ya weirdo," Eric replied with a violated look.

"Hope is the anchor of the soul. But hope is not simply a wish. Hope is the certainty of the promises of the future that God has made."

Eric lit his smoke and with the first drag he gagged and vomited.

"Is that your passion," Todd chuckled.

"*Who are you?*" Eric asked the man with accusation.

"I am the way, the truth, and the life. All who have faith in me shall never perish, but have everlasting life."

Todd's jaw hit the ground. He was creeped out. He wanted to run off, but he couldn't. With a little deductive reason, Todd concluded that Jesus Christ was standing in front of the two of them.

"Eric! It's Jesus!" Todd whispered with bulging eyes.

Jesus took a sip of wine from the bottle then held it out to Eric.

"This might be a little better for you."

Eric took a sip and handed it back to Jesus.

"Now I say to you Todd and Eric, may this be an instance of communion with the love and beauty that God has spilled out to you. May it fill you with hope. May it communicate to you the passion of God's love for all of humanity. This is my blood, poured out for you."

Jesus handed Todd the bottle.

"How should I address you?"

Eric wasn't sure if he should believe, or disrespect the man. Something spoke truth about the man standing in front of him, and Eric felt transcendent in the moment. He was beyond all the sensual pleasures of life. The cigarette held no appeal.

"Address me as Lord, brother Eric."

"Well Lord, thank you," Eric said with a smile.

The bottle went around again. Eric drank until he was full. In a slight haze of drunkenness, the three walked down the street headed towards the ocean. The weather was perfect, 78 and sunny, an ocean breeze. Peace was in the air, and on that day, the Prince of Peace was walking with Todd and Eric. They looked toward the future, or at least Todd and Jesus did. Eric still stared at the ground a lot. There was no expectation of the three parting ways. They seemed to find unity at a moment's notice. Todd was captivated by who he was with. Eric had no intention of bailing of Todd. It seemed the two mental patients had set foot unto a journey with Jesus. Now they were headed to the ocean.

"So why are you here?" Eric asked the Lord.

"Was it not told that I would return?"

"But why me? Why us?"

"Faith, righteousness. They're both fading."

By the time they made it to the beach, light was fading, and evening twilight had set in. The people on the beach lived in spiritual ignorance. Salvation was a term that only meant mortal preservation to these people. Comfort from the world they lived in left them numb to transcendental passions. Some of the hippies on the beach that night were talking spiritual transcendentalism. They were smoking weed, and the well-behaved ones sipped on tequila. Surfers and hippies were building bonfires on the beach and playing guitar, sitting, and talking, but ignored the role God played in all of it. They had desires for the higher pleasures in life like peace and health on a global scope, and they lost sight of their eternity. They tried their best to transcend beyond this mortal realm, ever changing without religion. They lacked the tools to reach the world of their visions. Ultimately, they were too passive, too ideal. They ignored the relationship between soul and Creator. The aggressive ones lacked virtue and piety. But what marked the assertive ones? Diligence? But to what end? Could this world see faith and passion as real and unified objects?

With the night air before them, they communicated with the power of the ocean as its breeze blew in the waves. The backdrop of indigo was illuminated with gold dots of stars, but the world was not praised. Just merely enjoyed and appreciated. There was little the Lord could do for the people who he only wanted to observe. He needed souls to participate, worship, and give thanks. He was not sure these were his believers, his chosen people. There was a loss of integrity in the world, particularly of those in positions of power and luxury. Without integrity nothing was sacred. If nothing was sacred, there would be no integrity. With Todd and Eric in tow, Jesus was focused on finding the epicenter of soul in this country that once claimed fearless faith.

"Let us go into the canyonlands."

Chapter 3: Canyon Spirit

Jesus was with his schizoaffective and acid-dosed friends at the Greyhound station in East LA. The Lord told Eric and Todd to leave their bags behind. They would need nothing, for as Henry David Thoreau has said, "A man is rich in that which he can afford to do without." They were headed to the Grand Canyon, and the Colorado River. The hour was early. Morning twilight was setting, in but the air and sky were still dark. East LA was crowded and noisy, folks walking around in poverty and despair, looking for some kind of light to guide the way. The three men boarded the bus for Grand Canyon National Park, largely unnoticed. Some passengers were getting off at stops along the way. Some were just trying to leave LA behind.

With everyone aboard, the bus started rolling. It took a few hours to make it out of the city, and by that time, the sun had risen high above the horizon. The desert was a vast expanse of orange light and blue skies as the bus rolled down the highway. Todd and Eric sat beside each other, and Jesus sat across the aisle in the same row. Behind them was an Hispanic woman in her mid-twenties, weeping.

"What troubles you?" Jesus asked as he turned around to face her.

They knew not the true sympathy of Christ just a day ago. Jesus wished to heal whatever pain and suffering he could. The innocent, and victims of evil were his lambs, and he was determined to shepherd anyone willing to follow.

"What troubles you?" he asked.

"I'm pregnant... and I can't raise this child," she replied weeping. Her tears were that of someone lost. She hated what she was on her way to do but, she felt like she had no option. She couldn't bring this child into the world only to give it the trials, pains, and troubles of an impoverished life. Killing was beyond her, especially her own flesh and blood, or at least once she thought that. But, now she was on her way out of Los Angeles to get an abortion, and try to start over.

"Dear, have strength. Let the Lord be your guide."

"That hasn't seemed to work so far." She mumbled as she wiped a tear from her eye. "I'm going to get an abortion. There is nothing more I can do."

"So far? Theresa, you have not followed the truth. That is not how you got to these circumstances."

Theresa was getting a little haughty.

"Have integrity. Give the child up for adoption. Someone out there can give the care you cannot. Do not kill your own flesh and blood. Do not deny the world the gifts this child has to offer."

Theresa cut loose. She wept, sobbing hard. Emotions of fear and regret pierced through her. She needed God more than anything. Tears streamed down her face as she was riding out the waves of depression and heartbreak. She felt the power of Christ in her soul. It brought her comfort. Divinity spoke reason to her passions. Jesus took her hand.

"Peace be with you, my dear," he said, holding her hand, and left the woman alone to contemplate life.

The bus was hot inside, but with windows down a breeze blew about. Eric witnessed something. He saw soul. The broken finding direction through the strong. Before, soul appeared to Eric as a commodity, like the number of surf boards or cups of coffee. But, there was quality *and* quantity. Todd was thinking a bit differently than Eric. A cycle of life, faith, vision, and afterlife ran through his mind. The tools functioning in each phase of the cycle are contemplated as we negotiate the obstacles of life. The idea of comfort facilitated the idea of happiness. Maintaining good health appeared as a personal responsibility. The idea of a utilitarian world made sense to the righteous, the principle of the most good to the most people, and doing good for the sake of doing good. But somewhere along the way someone got robbed, and we all settled for immediate gratification. The strong took advantage of the weak, meek, and mild. Righteousness was neglected, and evil grew into a thief robbing value from life.

Eric seemed to have lost to industry, and the capitalism that provides comfort, but degrades the soul. Stimulation and raw emotion replaced heritage and responsibility. The hip and simple laid in the crux between the natural man and titans of industry. In more archaic times, the idea of abortion wasn't an issue. People simply raised their kids with little question. Now, the ideas of society and environment establishes more implications to raising a child. The means of sustaining life wasn't at a cyclic high. We are no longer hunter-gatherers. We are suppliers and consumers. We lost sight of taking pleasure in the service you provide the world, perpetuating the good. As some who do and don't follow the Lord's teachings to make the world work, the grace and blessing of their talents-shared is the love-spread. It's what Christ tried to spread through the world with his words and teachings of God and the

Holy Spirit. Eric never considered the greater consequences of abortion before, the pain for the mother, the loss to the world, all of it. He always considered it just an easy way out of raising a child. After seeing what Christ could do for the lost, life seemed a bit more sacred to the hipster who sacrificed his own sanity on a dare. He was deep in contemplation. Then it began.

"I feel like I've been put on a shelf," Eric started. "You know, a keen observer and nothing more. What am I to be? Passion? I guess observing beauty is a passion of mine. Beautiful coffee and beautiful music seem to be my passions. But what about soul?"

Jesus leaned across the aisle and said,

"Eric this might sound heavy, but the world is not to live in us, as we live in the world. True fulfillment comes through a relationship with God and the presence of God. We all have been given gifts, skills, and talents, and we are all to produce fruits of the Holy Spirit which are love, joy, peace, patience, kindness, goodness, and faithfulness. Growth takes time. Find your gift and be fruitful."

Todd was contemplating his own thoughts.

"But what are the definitions of base and health?"

"Arthritis, maybe?"

"Huh?"

Eric was lost.

"Don't go sungazing too much."

"Sounds reasonable," Todd and Eric replied in unison.

The sun began setting around the time the bus made a stop for dinner. The hour was about 9:00 PM. The "when" and the "why" for the intermission were of importance: food in the hour of hunger. On the other hand, Christ was transcending. For him, the "when" and the "why" were not important. All that held weight for him in that transcendent moment was the "what," the Holy Spirit. The day was burning through its cycle. The men, women, and children ate simply to sustain their health in a crumbling world. Quick- service roadside food lacked the time, love and integrity of homemade food at the dinner table. Good meat and raw produce were hard to come by. Everything had its price in this capitalist market which our survival has come to depend on. To Jesus, the world seemed to sacrifice quality in the name of money and convenience, just like Theresa. It seemed convenient to abort the pregnancy. Quality and appreciation for the good of the world were cut back to save time and money. Two thousand years ago, he was the blood paid to validate the creation of man and our disobedience to God. Jesus became our righteousness. He lived a life no one else could live, and died a death we all deserved to die. As time passed, the quality of love seemed to fade. Jesus was forgotten, and unholy things were done in his name. Love might not have been at an all-time low, but it was declining, depressing amidst its cycle through time. Jesus had two men with him who could see these things. Todd and Eric were surviving on the threshold of humanity. They felt something was sacred, and they yearned for the strength to hold and multiply that something. Todd knew the answer was with Christ. Eric saw the sacred integrity within mankind's responsibility to love one another within this broken world. They could comprehend what was going on, but it was a concept that was not easily accepted, admitting we are broken, each and every one of us. Two thousand years ago, Jesus came to teach us how to love each other, and enrich the quality of our lives, and our world, becoming our righteousness and only salvation. His teachings were being forgotten, and Todd and Eric were seeing the necrotic tissue of the world sink into a numb, emaciated form. The cause was a little mysterious to Eric, but Todd had long been accustomed to seeing the reason for our brokenness.

"What does the word 'base' mean? You used it in a philosophical sense," Eric asked Todd.

Jesus was listening to the men without giving them complete focus.

"It means to put your interests before your obligations because of greed or cowardice," Jesus piped up.

Todd and Eric dwelt on the words for a while. Todd was victim of such an immoral crime. Episodes of mania drove him to robbery and heists. Amidst his illness, he put his greed before his obligations. It was the high of the action that drove him to such feats. He got off on stealing, but the world as a whole was growing more and more base as time went on. Obligations to God took second-seat to the interests of the self. Some say money is the root of all evil, but money is innocent. Money is only a means of purchasing. The true evil was the disregard for responsibility in the name of material reward. The responsibility to brothers, sisters, children, saving the weak, hungry, and disenfranchised was not base. However, doing things in the name of God or righteousness for a wealth of power and riches *was* base. It was not just the lost and immoral who were guilty of being base, but also the self-righteous who believed in their own opinions and their own authority above God and His authority. And, even humanitarians can forget their obligations to God and the full scope of what a person is capable of. The hippies in Santa Barbara were riding a sensual high. Jesus was after something transcendental, something beyond the flesh, and he hoped to spread that desire to the whole world.

"Who chased the hobbit out of the butcher shop?" Eric said in his sleep.

Jesus, Todd, and Eric were heading through the southwest along the canyonlands.

"This is the only expanse of rock like this in the whole world. Yet, among one of the least inhabited places on Earth. The Navajo and Hopi lived and loved in these canyons and deserts. Now it seems to just be tourists. There is something special about the spirit that lives here."

Painted rocks of mesa and canyon stretched along the road. Jesus was meditating on the sight of it. There was something out there he expected to find, and something out there he knew existed. He was the Son of God looking at his Father's creation. Thousands of years of tectonic divergence and weathering left an incredible sight that drew people to the canyonlands of the southwest every year. The sun was rising, and deep purple was penetrated by brilliant orange. The land contrasted the sky with a heavenly hue. Dynamic colors surfaced on the rocks, and deep into the body of the geology. God was the only one who knew the whole story behind their presence. It was vast with clarity, and enlightening to be in their presence.

The bus finally stopped at the Grand Canyon, and Todd, Eric, and Jesus got off.

"The mind should feel clear with such vastness. The world seems larger, and we seem to gain more from the great wilds of this

Earth. They let the frame of mind grow. Distractions in the periphery seem miniscule. This is a special place. Such a great expanse of rock! Keep your eyes on the horizon..."

Todd and Eric did just that. They were close to Lake Mead where paddlers get off of the river from running the Colorado through the Grand Canyon. They walked. The sun was bright and the air was hot and dry. It was much more peaceful than L.A. and Jesus' two disciples were adjusting to life outside of Buena Vista Behavioral Health Institution. They were now relying on Jesus' love, not the luck of their world. It was love, not luck, that they were seeking. Luck is a bit superstitious and obscure, dependent on the fate of misfortune God had planned for the unwise. Love was Holy and existed in the moment. Its inception was by the creation of the heart. It carried over through time with faith in truth. The landscape was transcending and spiritual, and the two were feeling the love. Jesus was their salvation. He was the faith that would sustain the spirit these men were after.

The walk was long, five or ten miles, and they were sweating in the dry heat by the time they reached the Colorado River. Todd kept a keen eye on the horizon, and Eric tended to look at his feet a lot. Todd was intrigued with where Jesus was leading him. Eric was just in a state of hopelessness and needed a leader. He knew not the miracles of salvation. His journey of spirituality was only beginning.

After walking the deep gulches between buttes and mesas of brilliant orange, red, and yellow rock, they came to a parking lot down by the river. Nothing else like it existed on earth, the canyonlands. For thousands of years Native Americans lived in these canyons, surviving on what could not be seen by the casual onlookers. The river and its water were sacred. Life revolved around what little moisture bled through the rocks, and fell from the skies, gouging its way down the ravines. Neither Todd, nor Eric had been there before but they could tell something was wrong when they came upon the take-out parking lot.

Only four people were there, where ordinarily droves of people are loading gear after running the river. Two Native Americans, Paasaakkii and Candillo, were tending a fire while two kayakers loaded their boats on the roof of a pickup truck. Paasaakkii and Candillo were on a vision quest. The paddlers kept glancing over at them. The Natives were playing flute and drum, chanting and dancing. They came to a special place to feel the spirit with open eyes and open ears in hopes to be shown a sign. The jam-funk-blues of The Odyssey was coming from the paddlers' ride. They were loose and giddy, tan and brazen from weeks on the river. They felt the spirit, but couldn't understand it with the same completeness Paasaakkii and Candillo did. They moved and hymned with the great flows of nature just as paddlers Nick and Rafa had done, but in an effort to become one with the Great Creator. They were looking for proof or direction, something to stand upon and have complete faith in. The kayakers turned down their music to feel the vibe Paasaakkii and Candillo were putting off. It was similar to the vibe that the river imparted. It was just felt on a different medium.

Jesus and his two disciples approached the Natives. Candillo looked impressed by the man before him. Paasaakkii wasn't sure what to think. With a bit of confusion on Candillo's face, he knelt in respect when Jesus walked up to him and his friend. Nick and Rafa smirked and giggled a bit.

"What living God do you worship, if not a man?" Jesus confronted the paddlers.

"Maybe a river!" Nick replied to bemuse the Lord.

"Your river has spirit, but so does a man. When you stand before judgement after your death, you will not be judged as a river. You will be judged as a man" Jesus remarked.

Jesus could see the way skill and talent rise up in the pride of a man, even in such frivolous acts as recreation. The men were fearless, or so they thought. They were fearless to the challenges they were familiar with. Nick and Rafa overcame powerful rivers in their crafts. But Paasaakkii and Candillo where fearless of the Spirit World. Wickedness would not sway them. They were Christians, or at least Candillo was.

Nick felt a little detested by Christ's convictions. Jesus was criticizing the man for what he believed in. The priceless intangibles of his soul and passions were cut down by a man who did not know him, yet claimed to be the path to salvation, the Living God. Jesus walked away and stood with Paasaakkii and Candillo, meditating on the flow of their souls. Energy and consciousness were cresting and receding with a calm magnitude. Insight and direction could be felt and conceived. The two Natives could feel that this was the true Messiah. They were sages, theologians, great mediums for the sacred and supernatural. This was not the second coming as theBbible described, and the sheer presence of the Lord was a little disturbing. Was this the rapture, or just a movement of salvation?

"Here is a gift. It is the highest gratitude I can show." Candillo laid a flute of bone and bird feathers in Jesus' hand then kissed his feet. "You are my savior. Without you I am damned."

"Thank you. *But what's more than this gift is your faith.* Candillo, I know you. Call on me *whenever* you need strength. I am here for you, but be like Nick and Rafa, too. Be fearless. Face great challenges with faith in me, and all things are possible. Have soul, have passion."

Candillo walked across the Mojave Desert from the lands of the Pasqua Yaqui in Central America. The walk took twenty days and Candillo refrained from eating along the entire trip. Paasaakkii came in similar fashion, walking from the lands of the Blackfoot tribe in Montana. He ate a button of peyote the day before arriving to the banks of the Colorado River and meeting Candillo. The spirit was moving within them. The vast landscape and broad horizon of the canyonlands have the ability of opening the mind, body, and spirit. It was sacred; the only place of its kind here on Earth. This was a different kind of church. The communion between nature and man was unpolluted and free flowing. With the right hands, a man could reach out and touch the spirit in righteous and supernatural ways. Fasting and a peyote trip offered visions of the Spirit World. The insight was not concrete. Much was left up to interpretation. Dangerous stuff when dealing with the supernatural. All that can be seen and felt under such influence may or may not be real, or true, or righteous. It can be the Devil's playground and a quick and dirty way of getting lost. Not everything seen in a hallucination is mere illusion. Sometimes those visions are moved by forces unknown and misunderstood by the one on their quest. A vision's meaning and influence can bring good, or it can bring bad, for real.

Jesus reflected.

"Can I call some of these people evil? Or are they just distant? So many have gone off searching for their own way. So many are embracing the natural wonders of the world. The beaches, the rivers, the mountains, the canyons. Do they really feel unified with my Father in heaven, or is it just another way of getting high, a simple and *finite* pleasure? There are worse things. I suppose they're not bad, just finite, and maybe misleading. Maybe it was the music. Maybe it was the wanderlust. If they only knew the *infinite* joy, the *infinite* wisdom of my Father, maybe they would be more interested in a relationship with Him. That's all He really wants is a relationship. A little communication. A little obedience."

Everyone at the river's take-out found themselves in a blissful moment of reflection. They were all lost in their heads, amidst a moment of ethereal peace. Did Jesus say those things, or just think them?

"Where do we go next?" Todd asked.

"Glastonbury," the Lord replied.

"What's in Glastonburry? *Where is* Glastonburry?"

"Music, The Odyssey."

Chapter 4: Phoenix to Stuttgart

The walk to Phoenix International airport was long and hot. The nights were cold. It took three days and three nights to reach on foot. They never stopped for food or water and kept moving the whole time. Once Jesus, Eric, and Todd got through security at the airport, they slept at the gate for a few hours. Eric had vivid dreams of the crucifixion while he laid resting. The pain and torture were at the forefront. It was not peaceful. He gained insight to the sacrifice Jesus made for mankind, giving his mortal life to resurrect the souls of sinners. Todd laid fast asleep with a Bible in his hand.

After a few hours they boarded their flight. The day was beautiful as they walked the gangway out to the airplane. A sweet breeze blew across the desert, harmless in its way. Dry heat blowing in the morning sun. Blue skies and soft bright light. The pilot checked all of his instruments, and the plane headed down the runway. As the craft lifted to the sky, a young woman was frantic.

"What fears do you keep?" The Lord asked.

"I don't wanna die!"

"On this thing?"

She nearly screamed.

"Do not fear your mortality. There is life after death for all who believe in me. We all pass on sooner or later."

She wiped the tears from her face. Jesus wanted to give her a hug but it was kind of impossible while sitting on an airplane. The four-hour flight to the east coast went on with a little turbulence, and the young lady winced with every bounce. Jesus held her hand, and she felt comforted. The Spirit was with the Lord. Anyone near him could feel it. An aura of peace fell upon all he consoled. He had a way of making the brutal truth a bit more bearable. Reality didn't seem so hateful. Eventually the connecting flight landed in Newark, New Jersey. The layover was short, and after an eight-hour flight they got off in Stuttgart, Germany.

"Ever been on a plane before?" Eric asked Todd.

"Nope." Todd replied

"What kept you so cool on the flight?"

"Some say I am fearless in His love."

The weather in Stuttgart was cloudy. Old German homes lined the streets just away from the airport.

Jesus asked Eric, "Now seems like a good time for food and coffee. Will you two join me?"

"Damn straight, uh I mean, darn tootin!'"

"Come, let's break bread."

Eric looked at the Lord a bit sideways but raised no question. Todd just whispered to Eric, "It's a Holy way of saying 'Let's eat'."

The groovy vibes of The Odyssey played in their minds as they walked about in search of food and coffee. The air was sweet, and it was beginning to feel more like a luxurious adventure than a mission trip as they strolled through Stuttgart in early summer. Eric and Todd were taken by the novelty of their setting. The landscape and the architecture were fresh and new. Its secrets were still untold. There was beauty and docile mystery about the town. Old wooden houses with German-style rooves, and German-style walls lined the street hiding tall gardens. Jesus was people-watching as he walked along. He could feel the spirit of the place. Todd's excitement was muffled by the medication. Mania and delusions of grandeur were subdued with pharmaceuticals. Eric gazed through sunglasses on the day, and tried not to feel hollow for the Lord was with him. It helped. The three trudged along until they came to Shwartz Café. They walked in. Two backpackers were the only guests in the place. Plenty of natural light illuminated the room. The Lord was intrigued. He saw opportunity as he overheard their conversation.

"Where is the next place we can see The Odyssey?" Kyle asked Beathan.

"They're playing in Munich in five days," Beathan replied.

Beathan's long, thick, black hair was braided into pigtails and hung down below his beard.

"My aunt lives in Munich. We can stay with her."

"I thought you were Scottish?" Kyle questioned.

"I'm a Bavarian-Druid, Beer and mushrooms, you know."

Beathan grinned with a bit of pride at his own words.

"America isn't the only melting pot, Kyle. You Americans think Europe is still a place of pure blood. My mother's side of the family is from Munich, Bavaria. My Father is a Pagan from the Scottish Highlands. I grew up hunting red deer, drinking dark beer, and dabbling with psychedelic mushrooms. Vison quests and the quest for the Great Spirit. A natural mystic."

"It would have done you well to chase a few girls in that time," Kyle tactfully responded.

"Eh, you can't see it. My passions are a bit more Earthy. It takes a certain heart to harmonize with what sustains health in the heart and the head. Maybe you should hunt a bit more, or at least eat a few mushroom caps in the Highlands."

"I've killed more deer than you know. But, the thirst for blood never polluted my passion for women."

The thrill of the chase existed in both men, but the fruit of the harvest laid at opposite ends of the spectrum for the two, ranging from love to death. Kyle was a free spirit from the mountains of western Pennsylvania. He hunted a little bit but loved skiing and hiking more than slaughtering animals or dabbling with mushrooms, for that matter. It didn't mean he was abstinent from psychedelic drugs. Kyle liked the pot-bud. He smoked it daily. Mushroom-rituals distanced Beathan from smoking habitually, but the Bavarian Druid kept a steady diet of red meat and dark beer. The bratwurst, potato salad, and dark lager before him were evidence of his intrinsic diet. It left him brawny with a deep throaty voice. His Scottish tongue broke through heavier when he had a few beers in him. Both men had given up the ties of society to chase the band called The Odyssey all over Europe, ending at the Glastonbury Music Festival at the end of summer.

When Beathan caught sight of Jesus he lowered his brow.

"Someone thinks he's Christ," Beathan muttered to Kyle.

The Lord leaned over and said,

"I think, for I am."

Todd was shaking his head with disbelief. He was enraged that no one could believe the Son of Man was before them, and he just wanted to explode. Normally he would rant endlessly, talking so long and fast that it would drive a man nuts. But in his rage, Todd was lost for words. He held back his thoughts and actions for sheer respect of the Lord's presence.

"*My* spirit is from the highlands. What say you be my savior, *Jesus?*" Beathan mocked.

"Yes, the Spirit. You believe good is good, yet you spend much time alone as Kyle has seemed to say. Man was not met to be confined to himself. I am a mark of humanity, The Spirit of the human, not the spirit of rotten trees and moonlight like your mushrooms have given to you."

Beathan was getting short tempered. The Lord was testing him.

"You know some philosophers called me a Utilitarian. Would you believe a philosopher?"

Kyle just sat back and grinned. "Don't test the Lord," Kyle sarcastically remarked, unsure if the man next to

him was really Jesus Christ, or just some lunatic.

"Please eat," the Lord said, and multiplied the food sitting before Beathan in that very moment.

Beathan's eyebrows raised and his eyes bulged. It was like the story of the fishes and loaves. The food kept coming. It was of miraculous, endless supply. Beathan sat back in his chair after he ate his fill.

"I have no enemy with you, that is for sure. I just wonder, why might God have a son?" said Beathan after finishing his meal of bratwurst and potato salad.

"Each spirit of creation has a mark of divinity, no? What say I am the divine mark of man, The Son of God, sent to die in your place for your eternal salvation? Wouldn't you like to call a man like Kyle 'Son'?"

"That's a powerful remark, *son,*" Kyle chipped in at Beathan.

"Okay, grand. What do you want with me? What are you trying to prove?"

"Spiritual revelation. The path to a better life. Truth. Peace. I want you to guide me."

"You're the Son of God. Why do you need *me* to guide *you*?"

"Your kind is dear to my heart."

"You understand I am a pagan?"

"Then maybe you will see the world differently. The Living God is with you; Spirit beyond the mystical affections of art, philosophy, and nature. Guide me to the Odyssey. It's the epicenter of your kind."

The five of them left the coffee shop together when they were finished eating. They were on their way to the train station, and eventually Munich to see The Odyssey. Meanwhile, Nick and Rafa were off to Africa to chase another big river, the Zambezi.

The Zambezi River is huge and powerful whitewater, second toughest river to kayak in the world. Far to the north of the Zambezi lies the Sahara Desert, a vast expanse of dry wasteland not fit for man. Out in the desert, heathens were fasting, feeding the passions of delirium and superstition in hopes some sign would come to them, a sign of a higher power, a sign of direction, some kind of teaching. They would be disappointed on their vision quest. The symbol of love and knowledge had already come to our world 2,000 years ago. But, the intrinsic desire to pioneer faith and find greater meaning in life never departed from human instinct. Every seeker yearned to develop their own *"Way."* Nick and Rafa were not of the superstitious type. Their passion was the whitewater. The desert-fasters' passion was draped with mystical fallacy. Fasting and sun gazing left the soul dry and withered; hammered and rotten raw. Times were tough and lost souls were searching for direction. The pains and challenges of this world gave the desert-fasters little hope of a Living God. Nick and Rafa chased the embodiment of God through their whitewater experiences. And at the end of each run, the soul felt delight with a sense of joy and accomplishment, but it was not a feat of humanity. They knew that once again, they were at the hands of something more powerful than themselves, but Nick and Rafa had faith only in themselves to carry them past the obstacle at hand. Sooner or later, they might run into an obstacle they couldn't paddle through. They might need the help of a higher power. They would paddle twenty miles of class five and six whitewater before taking their crafts out on dry land, and leave the raucous swell of the river behind. But, not before feeling so alive as to be more human than human.

Chapter 5: Finding the Odyssey

Jesus and his disciples were on the night train between Stuttgart, Germany and Munich. Passing through the German Alps was breathtaking. High aretes carved out of the mountain by glaciers, with alpine forest just below the alpine tundra. Barren rock screeched high above the railroad tracks when the mountainous foothills breathed deep with deciduous forest. In the dimly lit coach car, Kyle was rolling a joint to smoke out on the caboose of the train. Beathan was swigging beers in the café car, and Eric was sound asleep sitting next to Jesus. They all were finding peace in their own way. Even Todd who quelled his mania and hallucinations by taking his meds and contemplating scripture, reading the Bible. Todd's method offered the most moderation. His passions could be held with a transparent soul. Though his mental disability predisposed him to be the most likely of the crew to be led astray, his method, his faith, anchored him more solidly into a comfortable reality than any of the rest. He accepted that he was part a broken race, obviously broken himself. But, the peace of mind he gained through spirituality, spirituality grounded in the evidence of the Living God, kept him pressing forward in a righteous way. It was his passion. Some might call him a heretic, but he was not obnoxious, a little abrasive at times, maybe, but no more than the New Age Spiritualists and hippies blind to the light of the Messiah. There seemed to be a mass movement of those types, the ones idolizing good vibes to no end, the ones that lacked the grace of salvation. Yes, they had passion, but so did Todd. Soul and passions were flowing amongst the disciples. There was common direction, but the roads to their destination took different turns for each of them. They all had an outlook to experience some music and connect with lost souls. They were untamed, yet kind. What could the word 'kind' mean? It's a homonym meaning of a peaceful way and also meaning of similar sort.

The disciples were not all of the same kind, but all had kindness in their hearts. They searched for that beautiful-something that spoke to the soul. They were all walking different spiritual paths. They looked for something more in life. They each had their brushes with hell. Beathan, knowing blood and brutish ways more than love. Todd, suffering from the mental burdens of schizoaffective disorder. And, Kyle and Eric just wandering, looking for their place in life. For some, the hells were tame. For some they were heavy. They searched for beauty, for power, for love. The answer for each quest could be found in Christ. His teachings proved to build a better world. As one reflects on life through the course of time, the advancement of comfort, convenience, and luxury could be seen. Unfortunately, original sin paved the way for a broken race. Vice led to greed and oppression. Many a seeker wished to transcend the burdens of this world through whatever pleasures they were destined to find. But not all of those pleasures were Godly. Not all of them made a better place. Those who God might call the salt of the Earth, ones who were vibrant and passionate, were not all believers. Jesus was out to bring the saltiest of dogs into the Kingdom of God.

Kyle smoked his joint on the caboose trying to make sense of things.

"Geeze. I just wanted to go backpacking. Europe and the Odyssey, ya know…. Then this… Jesus Christ asking me to guide him to *my* people."

It was heavy. Kyle felt lost. Maybe he was, but by how much, he was unsure. Likely, he was no more lost than most other people. He had spent most of his life on the road searching for something beautiful that made him feel whole. God? The Spirit? A companion? Maybe it was just time and place that he was searching for in life. Years ago, he spent his days chasing the Odyssey, eating LSD and snorting MDMA. The high felt beyond words, but it took him somewhere close to the frame of mind Eric was in these days. After the drugs wore off, he felt hopeless and helpless. Rolling on ecstasy made him feel at home. He felt in place with the crowd and the drugs. It felt like his purpose for living. Eventually, he saw through the high, and the augmented vision of reality. He laid off hard drugs, and found a little bit of the spirit. That little bit was not enough to make him feel like he knew where he was, or what he wanted be, but he started to feel whole. Maybe he wanted a woman, but the quick and dirty relationships he was making were not fulfilling. So, the road began calling to him. Out there, he felt like he was closing in on something tangible and righteous. It always seemed to be accompanied by good music. That's were his spiritual life was steadfast. That's where he felt alive. But Kyle was more than just good vibrations. And, the good vibes alone weren't enough to complete him. He felt a sense of constant exile, as though no matter where he traveled or what he did there was a piece missing in his life. He just didn't know what the missing piece was.

Kyle took another long drag off his doobie. The smoke tasted good, and he could feel the blood flow through his head and endorphins release in his brain. His eyes squinted, and he watched the foothills of the German Alps pass by in the moonlight. He knew exactly where he was, and where he was headed. How could he be lost? Or did he really know where he was headed? For the moment he did, so he felt in place.

"What of the end of life? I don't know where I'm headed, Heaven or Hell."

Then Kyle laughed at himself. He never thought judgement of the soul and an afterlife to be something real and valid. Now he was on a night train to Munich with Jesus to see a jam band and convert hippies to Christians. So many lost sight of their soul with a dive into psychedelic drugs.

"Is this Jesus guy gonna tell my people to 'Just say no' to drugs!?"

Kyle shook his head in disbelief, then laughed at the thought. The smoke and deep thoughts were getting him excited. He rubbed his temples in slow circles trying to get back to the Zen-like state he was in. The breeze from the train was blowing back his dirty blond hair. The moonlit hills of Germany were breathtaking, and the moment was peaceful.

"This is what life is about," Kyle thought to himself with a smile.

He felt in place and wanted nothing more. With the presence of the Lord weighing on him, his thoughts progressed towards death and judgement once more. But this time Kyle did not feel perilous. Instead he contemplated Heaven. What would such a place be like? Good smoke, free travel, and live music? Maybe. Why else would he believe such a place would exist? His mind eased back into a state of Zen and he stayed out on the caboose for a long time.

The sun was rising as the train was closing in on Munich. Beathan was waking up to a groggy morning. A long night of drinking dark Bavarian lager progressed to a dreary morning arrival into the Munich train station. He grabbed his backpack, and Kyle came through the railcars to meet his four companions on the platform. The train was mad confusion with people looking for luggage and getting off the train. It was like herding cattle through the turnstiles for slaughter. It was an introverted moment. Those departing couldn't be worried about anything other than themselves. The moment of mindless-trudging passed, and Jesus and his four disciples were reunited as the train rolled away. The thought of drinking, smoking, or chasing women was pushed to the back burner. The men weren't happy about the sacrifices they were making but they felt a calling to the greater good. They felt a desire for the higher pleasures in life. The Spirit was with them.

"Can we *at least* get some coffee?" Eric whined.

"Eric, if you're going to ask questions, ask them with a little integrity," Jesus pleaded.

"I'm *trying* to grow a spine."

Eric looked like he just got punched in the face. The young hipster scratched the short hairs on his head. Even his sunglasses couldn't hide the disdain and detachment. They trudged along through the dreary Munich sunrise. The skies were cloudy, and the air was dank. A soft breeze blew dew and remnant-raindrops off the trees. The pattering of water on the landscape was comforting. The men needed something ethereal to pull them together as one. The presence of Christ was not enough for the whole clan. Beathan was groggy and dismissive. Kyle was coming down off the smoke. But, Todd was bopping along with keen perseverance. He was examining everything in sight. Landscapes, people, buildings. He was looking for something, he just wasn't sure what that something was.

"How do you know who to help and who to ignore?" Todd asked the Lord.

"You help those who want helped. You ignore those who wish to be ignored."

"Do they always know which side of the ball they're on?"

"Not always. If a man makes himself vulnerable and asks for help, he deserves the assistance. Becoming vulnerable, alone, doesn't qualify a man to be blessed. Folly can make you vulnerable, but folly is not a request for help. When a man puts down his armor and asks to be guided by the Father, Son, and Holy Spirit, he is destined to be saved. Seek, and ye shall find. If a person doesn't believe in me, what propensity do I have to bless them. Pride has a way of confusing a man about faith. What we have, we have because of the Father. Having a humble heart gives a clearer vision to the real-self, and a better understanding of your real-worth. It sheds light on true needs."

"What of a man who is always on guard?"

"One day he will need help, and if he is too bold to let help come, he will have a reckoning."

Todd thought about those words. *"A reckoning will be had."* Todd had been there. Stealing cars and robbing houses. Then prison: the jungle behind bars. His elusiveness had been crushed. He realized he was no longer invincible. For a man with schizoaffective disorder, the reckoning was earth-shattering. He could see his insanity. He needed some degree of normality. He felt helpless. Within his dither, Todd opened his Bible. It was an experiment for him. If he opened his heart to Jesus, would God find him? Would he find salvation within his hell? Maybe that was the starting point, looking for humanity. Love, kindness, and salvation.

It was hard to get a good read on the people of Munich in the early hours of a workday. Everyone was off to the office, and didn't seem to express much soul in positive or negative directions. Everyone just appeared to be burdened by the 'work to live' motto. Working to live was not living. It may have been a means of finding something worthwhile about life, but dollar signs got in the way of truly being free and happy. We are not meant to be lovers of money. It only provides emptiness, just as Todd had felt empty in jail. It was not the path to enlightenment or fulfillment. That was hid in the ability to do more with less. Yet, people seemed to be set on achieving convenience and luxury.

Beathan and Eric had been there, given countless opportunities to make the most of richness in wealth and culture, yet blinded by the superstition that stimulating the self with sensual pleasures would make a life worthier of living. Beathan had been on hunts that tested his will, strength, and knowledge, deep in the wilderness for days; easily a spiritual experience. But, when the hunt was over, Beathan paid no mind to giving thanks to God for this great Earth, and the experiences he had been given. He ignored the Great Spirit that set forth the dynamic harmony of the wilderness (or at least never recognized an ultimate, divine being for creating it all). Far too much attention was focused on the sensual stimulation of the high country and the adrenaline rush of the hunt. He was blind to the forces that created it. Over time, it just became a blood-thirsty chase instead of a spiritual experience.

Eric tasted some of the best food and drink Santa Barbara had to offer, and thanklessly, but what became of it? A boost to the ego, and a trip down the path that rotted his feelings of hope and humanity. He had a rough ride on the LSD that led him to Buena Vista Behavioral Health Clinic. An overload of sensual stimulation drained him of soulful living. He was empty. Completely exhausted. He couldn't even fix his eyes on anything that had higher meaning than a pack of cigarettes in his pocket, and the ability to put one foot in front of the other. Now they were walking down the streets of Munich on a dreary Tuesday morning just a bit lost.

Beathan took the lead. He was the only one familiar with the city. Jesus was beside him. The atmosphere the two shared was uneasy to say the least. A short-tempered buzz of anxiety could be felt flowing out of Beathan towards the Lord. His heart was restless, and he couldn't find peace towards the Son of God. The other disciples followed close behind. Kyle and Beathan had backpacks, long hair, and beards giving them the mark of vagabonds, travelers, wanders. Todd and Eric had nothing but the clothes on their back. They were a little underdressed for the climate, and the tension between Beathan and Jesus was bothering all three of them. Todd shivered a bit.

"Cold?" Beathan asked.

"Yeah," Todd replied.

With a smug grin, Beathan interjected.

"Just lets you know you're alive!"

Todd trudged along, awakening more and more with each passing city block. Birds sang, and the sun cut through the clouds and fog, warming the morning air. Old houses lined the blocks as they passed, moving away from the train station and business district.

"So, what do you know about The Odyssey? I mean, I didn't think the Lord grooved on hippy music."

"Is the music good?"

"None better!"

"Does it make you feel alive?"

"Oh yeah!"

"There's a story about three men. The first believed in God with complete fear. He did nothing more with life than, work, eat and sleep. He was a good worker, only ate kosher food and only slept at night. The second rebelled against God and indulged in all sensual pleasures and perversion. He had no depth. When he sat in reflection or meditation, he felt nothing good. His soul was completely empty. The third lived to connect with the world around him. He did not over-indulge, and he was not a slave to fear. Through the relationships he made, and the impressions he developed, be built a spirit of righteousness and passions, true love for all. The Odyssey can be seen as an over-indulged sensual pleasure, or it can be seen as something that builds a spirit of love and righteousness. It can strip the soul of burdens, catalyze growth and beauty, but being a slave to the music because of fear or resentment to the rest of the world keeps people from achieving their potential. The catalyst of *this* music conditions its listeners to be the salt of the Earth. But man cannot live on music alone. People become righteous through grace and God. Through faith and repentance. Through Christ and the cross. I just hope we can make people see that. Kyle, did you always believe in me?"

"Well seeing is believing, and your real enough to shake your hand."

"That's not what I asked."

Kyle repositioned his focus to the real question, and began explaining himself.

"Throughout my life I believed. But to say I *always* believed would be wrong. I have had my moments of weakness when I felt there was no proof of heaven, or God, or a messiah…"

Kyle was a believer who did not worship. He did not regularly take the time to praise the Lord and remember his teachings. At the time of rapture, he would not be one of the church that Christ would return for, like scripture had said. Like many, he wanted proof. He wanted the goodness that salvation promised. He forgot that there was balance required in the life that was his, and the faith in the Spirit that would save him. He liked Jesus, but wasn't sure what God wanted from him. He was never taught that all humans are sinners. We are all born of a broken race, a race that rebelled against God eons ago, and our only salvation from spiritual-death was faith in Christ, and repentance of our sins. It would take discipline to become righteous, and not in the hip sense. It would take discipline from lust and perversion to become a better man, but he couldn't see reasons for making such sacrifices before. He could not see the changes the world needed. He could not become that change which he could not see. The beliefs he had in his weaker moments were gritty and Earthly. He hunted for something that could have proven a higher power to him. He was chasing ghosts. He was looking in the wrong places, and hope became elusive. He was finding faith in the will-of-the-self instead of the guidance of God. A simple life with pleasure in work-done eluded Kyle. He needed guidance, and he needed to spread the word. The hope those things brought were all that could make him feel whole. We were not created to be distanced from God. We were not created for a lifetime of hard work. Those things were merely punishments for rebelling from the Creator. Like us all, he wished he didn't have to work. Most of his life was spent chasing after music, and the community that music derived. It made him feel good but it was incomplete logic. Brokenness shrouded salvation from the hip community. It was not free from lust or gluttony, sex or drugs. What it had was a common wavelength that could reach so many who felt lost and empty. It made them feel alive. But God said that it was not in this life that we truly live, but in the life we have in Heaven. The music-community made people feel so alive with its sensual stimulations that more than this could not be imagined. Maybe people didn't want to imagine that there could be more than this. But, the music brought people together. Their hearts were primed to share God's blessings with each other. They just needed a divine savior. Guidance. Direction. They needed the Son of God to bridge the gap between man and God.

Chapter 6: Aunt Freida's

With a knock on the door, Beathan was greeted by his Aunt Frieda. She had on lederhosen and her blond hair was braided into pigtails.

"Gat's güt?" She greeted her nephew with a smile. "And who are your friends!?"

"Just a couple of us in town to see a band."

"Ahh. Beathan, you have always been a nomad with your hunting and your music. Come in."

Beathan led the way, dropping his bag at the door and all the men went into Aunt Frieda's cottage. Savory smells rolled in from the kitchen. The wooden walls and floors were marred with character from years of living. The place was small. The five men all sat down. Some in the kitchen, some in the living room.

"Can we stay the night?" Beathan asked.

Flustered, Aunt Frieda replied.

"I don't have beds for all of you!"

"We can sleep on the floor."

Aunt Frieda looked over the travelers before giving an answer.

"Tell me a little about yourselves, first."

"Well, this is my buddy, Kyle," Beathan started.

"I'm from America. Beathan and I met on a camping trip in the Scottish Highlands. I needed a guide and he was working for an outfitter. We talked about music and shared a common interest in a band, The Odyssey. I've been backpacking western Europe for 10 months now, and life is good."

"What part of America are you from, Kyle?"

"Pennsylvania."

"Well, where have you been in the past ten months?"

Kyle began listing places as if Frieda wouldn't be able to understand the ethos of what he has experienced in his travels.

"Portugal, Spain, France, Great Britain. Beathan and I flew in to Stuttgart together after our trip in the Highlands."

"Were you friendly with the women in Spain? They have quite the reputation," Frieda remarked with the same smug grin Beathan wore once before.

Kyle turned red and got quiet.

"Ohh, I see," Frieda continued.

"Yeah... I got herpes while I was in Spain."

Beathan and Todd tried to hold back their laughter. Eric just looked cross at the two men's reaction.

"That's not funny guys!" Eric flared.

"I know, I know," Beathan admitted.

Kyle's response was amusing, but to say that it was comical would be wrong.

Beathan turned to Jesus.

"Is *that* why a man is not supposed to have sex before he is married?"

"Abstinence is safer than lust..."

"Not for the psyche," Beathan rebutted.

"Hm… Humans are supposed to mate for life. Sex and love are more meaningful that way. Something about us as creatures. Sentience, most likely. But, sexual illness is definitely a type of punishment for being a whore."

Frieda looked a little confused about the banter between Beathan and the Lord. It was the first time Jesus spoke since he entered her house.

"Who *are* you?" Beathan's aunt asked.

Before Christ could say a word, Beathan rebutted.

"It's Jesus. He's back," Beathan said, unimpressed.

Frieda laughed with a closed mouth.

"Lust steals from the respect that love delivers, the respect that commitment delivers. It makes us wanton of immediate gratification, and deprives patience from the soul."

They all sat quietly in Freida's living room, and Aunt Frieda gazed at Jesus with wanting eyes. No one said a word about it out of respect for Aunt Frieda. Then she shook her head and brushed her hair back. She was not Christian or even religious. She *was* quite the beer drinker though. She lusted for the handsome man in a white robe but refused to flirt with him. Something unfamiliar nipped at her conscience, and kept her from putting the moves on the Lord. He was handsome with long dark hair, glowing skin, and a clean white robe. Even on the surface, Jesus was quite the man, but it was his wisdom that really warmed one's heart. Intelligence is sexy. That is without a doubt. But a wise man is not wise by making dumb decisions. The road a traveler walks is one open to new experiences, but Kyle was proof that not all new experiences along the road are rewarding. Christ was wise to that snare. This woman was not to be his bride. That privilege was reserved for the multitudes who praise and worship him.

"Would anyone like a beer?"

To everyone's surprise, Christ said he would. Then, the rest of the gang asked for a beer as well. Freida poured six mugs of beer and passed them out to everyone and kept one for herself. It was dark Bavarian lager.

"I see why the monks enjoy it," Jesus said with a smile.

Eric sipped slowly as if to critique the brew. The expression on his face said that he was deciphering something in his mind. Beathan just opened his gullet, swilling down large quantities of beer. Todd and Kyle drank in a little more usual fashion.

"I didn't think Christ drank?" Frieda asked.

"I drink. I don't drink until I am intoxicated. There's a line there. I'm just enjoying a frothy, amber liquid. I'm not getting drunk."

"Can't a man savor some flavor?" Eric asked smartly.

The crowd didn't know whether to laugh or be insulted. The words carried just enough weight to be valid, but coming from the hipster, they were whiney and stereotypical.

"It's okay, Eric. A man will always be criticized," Christ consoled his follower. The words were of little comfort to Eric. He always wore the criticism of a hipster, but his ego told himself that he was better than the critics. Still though, having refined taste was not enough to make one person better than the next. Fine taste and hip fashion were the trademarks of the hipster identity. Eric tried so hard to connect to those two icons that he forgot to be grateful and live for the moment. He tried so hard that he took one drug too strong for his mind and was left hollow. He was rebuilding his soul. The presence and guidance of the Lord helped construct passions that were a bit more righteous than they were refined.

Jesus had one beer then asked if he could take off his sandals and lay down. The gang made room for him, and Kyle and Beathan kept drinking all night. Todd and Eric had a few, but not enough to get intoxicated. Eric was still depressed. The hallucinations stopped weeks ago, and the delusions they brought on had subsided, but he had a hard time feeling like he belonged where he was at. He felt there were people better fit for the feat he was taking on with Jesus and the rest of the disciples. He didn't have enough faith in himself, but he was becoming grateful for the faith he could put in the Lord. Eric was thinking long and hard about something in the quiet hours after midnight. Eventually the thoughts became more than he could hold inside. He turned to Todd in the dimly lit room and asked with indifference,

"What lies do you blame?"

"Huh?"

The question was a bit random, and a little obscure. Todd was caught off guard. Eric asked again, this time directive.

"Well… lies of arrogance and haughtiness."

Todd found his confidence through the truth of the Lord. He wasn't a perfect son, having a mental disorder, a combination of schizophrenia and bipolar-mania. But, despite having a broken mind, the man was righteous, devoting his life to ministry in an unofficial way. Every broken soul he met, he did his best to advise them to seek the Lord. He taught them what the Lord had taught. He tried to be quick to listen, slow to speak, and slow to anger. Todd's passions were somber. His psyche was not. His mental disability was the mark of a broken race. He was destined to be torn from within, but did his best to help others escape their pains. And the only way he could deal with his tormented mind was through devout spirituality. He tried to help Eric in that groggy Munich night. Exoticism was replaced by desolation. Eric seemed to feel the hopelessness of obscurity melt away by the mission at hand. He did not know what waited for him in the afterlife, but the here and now was growing in his heart. Passion was beginning to take hold within Eric as he could see the strength that was steeled in Todd.

The next morning came with good spirits. Kyle was smoking a joint with his cup of coffee and Beathan was cooking eggs, potatoes, and sausage for the clan. Frieda opened the bathroom to anyone who wanted to freshen up, and Todd and Eric sipped tea with Christ on the back porch.

"What awaits in heaven?" Eric asked Jesus, interrupting the tranquility of a dewy morning.

"Your loved ones, times the best of the best, comfort, blessings, and splendor. Incredible worship with the forces of the Holy Spirit exploding from within. You're not just in a big armchair riding around on clouds."

That last line made Eric laugh. The thought of something as grand as heaven made Eric contemplate the broken and wicked ways of this world. Desire for deep thoughts were half the cause of eating the acid in the first place. Eric wanted to expand his mind, whatever that meant. Little did he know, he would expand it to the point of feeling empty and hollow. Brilliant minds are often riddled with despair and Eric was no exception. Eating the acid was not righteous, but the aptitude for growth thereafter created the possibility for a righteous living, something more humanitarian than hip, but it wouldn't be without the pains of privation and insight towards greed and corruption. Before, it was easier to just look away and sip his latte`. Now he couldn't help but focus on what was wrong with the world. Arrogance and haughtiness. Jesus was leading him somewhere righteous, but Eric couldn't help but judge the antagonists. Why would God make a man feel pain? Was it symbolic of all the hurt we cause? Was it more than punishment for our disobedience? Was he trying to resolve the pains of many men by means of only one man's pain? The world would not be saved until all knew the Lord's teachings and power. Eric was becoming a vassal of the Holy Spirit.

Kyle was about finished with his doobie when Todd walked into the kitchen.

"Wow." Todd exalted with a chuckle.

"What?" Kyle remarked with insecure accusation.

"The smell of pot and sausage. That's one heady morning," Todd said with a smile.

Beathan, Kyle, and Aunt Frieda laughed.

Soon Eric and Jesus came inside and everyone ate breakfast. Then, Eric began.

"When is this 'Odyssey' Concert?"

"They play in three days."

"What do we do until then?" Eric asked.

Chapter 7: The Park

The five of them spent the next three days people watching in the park. None of them went in empty handed. Eric kept a tall cup of coffee with him. Todd had a Bible. Jesus had a bottle of wine. Beathan had a six pack of Bavarian lager, and Kyle had a bag of weed. The focal point was not universal. Todd paid attention to those who looked troubled. Eric scrutinized those who appeared too sophisticated. Beathan was critical of those who were too happy. Kyle was the only objective one; a blank canvas to whatever Christ had to say about the other's opinions. It was a testament to human perception. For the most part, people are subjective with their opinions, displaying the ability to identify pain or weakness, but what isn't seen on the surface is the relativity of an individual's spirit. The modes of survival and mind sets of the billions of people on this planet are molded by genetics and the environment of existence. Those are not universal. What is universal to mankind is the ability to transcend the bounds of this world through Christian faith. It provides peace upon peace. It establishes hope on the promise of things yet unseen. Our concept of truth and reality are conditioned by our perception and experiences, but the belief in a higher power is the embodiment of the supernatural within the soul.

There was the young couple in the park, giggling and gazing into each other's eyes. Beathan couldn't think less of them.

"Look at them. What do you think will happen the first time they face adversity and suddenly life isn't happy-go-lucky?"

"Beathan what they have is special," Jesus started. "Don't diminish their joy just because it doesn't appear strong in a rough and tumble sort of way. Joy like that adds depth to the spirit. Don't think it shallow to feel love. It poses a goal, an objective to reach when times get hard. Without experiencing joy like they have, they wouldn't know why they should fight hard and make sacrifices to keep each other through thick and thin."

Beathan hushed, and kept to his beer for a while, enjoying the warmth of the sun shining down upon him. He looked over at Eric who was just shaking his head at some business man talking on a cellular phone.

"What a stiff! I bet he doesn't even know how to smile," Eric belittled the man.

"Being hip isn't the sole qualifier of merit, Eric. Maybe he's a provider. Maybe what he does keeps others healthy and honest."

Todd and Kyle didn't have much to say about anyone. Todd just kept looking at the few sullen faces that shuffled through the park looking lost and lonely. He wanted to approach them and tell them to keep the Lord in their heart, take delight in the fact that God loves you. But, it seemed to be more than Todd could do. There was something inside of him keeping him from going up to total strangers and sharing the Christian message of faith, love, and hope.

"Lord, why is love and assistance more than a man can give at times?"

Jesus didn't have to think too much before he answered.

"Pride, primarily. Judgement, complementary."

Todd just looked a little sideways at the Lord.

"A man puts much weight on what others think of him. Faith is something each person must find on their own. It's harder to bring someone to faith than it is to bring the self to faith. If a man predicts doubt over faith from the ones he tries to help, he senses that he will be judged, and his pride will suffer."

"Why are we people watching?" Kyle interjected.

"Every face tells a story," Todd replied.

"But we're not *hearing* their stories. We're just catching superficial impressions."

"*Very good*, Kyle." Jesus was impressed. "Come, let's walk."

The five men got to their feet with libations consumed. The head felt heavy and the feet felt new. The sun was bright, stifling the eyes, but the five men gazed upon the horizon where architecture met landscape. They began walking. They left the park and meandered through the city blocks of Munich, far away from where business and commerce held precedent.

All that Jesus and his pals could see were houses, bars, and cafés. Bavarian architecture of wood and thatch was appealing to the eye.

"Beathan, what makes these people so strong and jolly?" Jesus questioned.

"Beer and will power. These hills might have something to do with it too."

Jesus reflected on Beathan's words.

"A man once wrote a book about the way spirit varies from place to place. He said spirit to be dynamic and only understood through experience. The pleasure gained by experiencing a hard day's work, and a beer at the end of it, all energizes the consciousness into something unique. Strong and jolly."

"The place is growing soulless though. I'm proud to be a Highlander. I just come for the beer and maybe any, what's the American term? Cougars? Aunt Frieda might be running with for the weekend."

Kyle, Todd, and Eric tried to keep from laughing.

"What do you mean by soulless?" Jesus questioned.

"You're the divine one here. Do you really need me to explain it?"

"Well I guess I have to answer my own question. It seems like the material world is taking over the spiritual world. But, do you really think everyone in this city would prefer things over experiences?"

"I don't know. I see a lot of suits caught up in the money game."

"Well I guess it's a good thing that the five of us are out to attest the things money cannot buy," Jesus said with a grin.

The five of them walked quietly, each pondering their own thoughts. What was to be experienced? Eric was questioning that deeply, brooding over the ideology of empirical intelligibility. What Eric called soul was something that could be bought and sold in the marketplace. Those were his passions, but they were not holy or righteous. He could look to Beathan for something a bit more natural or mystical, but Beathan didn't have all the answers either. He knew something spiritual; the thrill of the chase and surviving the elements. His time spent hunting in the great wilds of the Scottish Highlands was diluted with fallacies of psychedelic drugs and pagan mysticism, yet his experiences were felt with passion. They were fascinating to recollect and contemplate. No matter the fallacy, they gave him hope and purpose. They were beautiful, gripping ideas that appeared to be filled with some kind of mystical wisdom. He felt visionary and prophetic to follow the spirit of the wild and the mystical delusions derived by the psychedelic drugs. There may be real things that the sane and sober never perceive, supernatural and spiritual things, but as Todd has come to learn, those things are best left to the care of God, Christ, and the Holy Spirit. Todd spent many a delusional day trying to smooth out the bumps of his disability. The hallucinations skewed his reality into a delusional compilation of thoughts and feelings that were anything but true or righteous. Todd needed the guidance of God to find out how to stand on the correct foot. Beathan didn't look to God. He tried to find signs and symbols from nature and make his own path. He was lost but didn't know it.

As Kyle walked, he took in the smells of the streets, and the sounds that pervaded the airways. To Kyle, the streets of Munich were one more beautiful landscape upon this great Earth. It was fresh and new. It added variety to his collection of experiences, and though it didn't present the challenges that build strength, that day did not fall short of building character. Character was found in the appreciation and gratitude each man felt within as he walked this blessed Earth. To Kyle it didn't matter what the man across the street looked like, for he knew that man played his part in making this world what it is.

"What it is…" Kyle coolly remarked at everyone's internal question: Why, and for what?

Chapter 8: Inca River

The Zambezi River isn't what one would call a warm up run. But, few people in this world paddle like Nick and Rafa. After paddling the Zambezi, they had their sights set on one bigger. The biggest. The Inca River. High up in the Andes Mountains of South America, raging water rushes down the craggy steeps attracting the bravest and most skilled of paddlers. Nick and Rafa were talking about getting spiritual. It's a term that dedicated outdoor enthusiasts understand. Getting spiritual was about achieving that feeling of Zen amongst the wildest, most adrenaline filled moments. Everything in the periphery melts away and you become lost in the moment. The world melts into one. The internal feels external, and the external is felt within. You become part of the rushing water, and the amplitude of your spirit matches the magnitude of the swell.

Far below the Inca River, in the rain shadow of the Andes Mountains, lies the Atacama Desert, the driest place on earth. Desert-fasters were chasing mystical hallucinations as they braved the extreme heat and dryness in privation of food. They removed the tangible fuel of the body, food, and looked for spiritual fuel. They were lost and they knew it. They were out there searching for a sign, something divine. They may have danced, or meditated, or sun-gazed, but they were ignoring the light that had already been given to the world: Jesus. They wanted something existential and transcendental, fresh and new. They wanted to be originals, pioneers in the field of salvation, but the One had already come, and his message was simple; spread his teachings of love and virtue, and he will return for his bride, the church, when the whole world over has learned this.

Some of those fasting had passed the ten-day mark. It's hard to say who got more spiritual in their days in South America. Pagan mystics would have their money on those out in the Atacama. The seasoned whitewater enthusiast would surely have their money on Nick and Rafa. But what to come of it? When the pinnacle is reached, where do you go from there? Some would say head in the opposite direction, comfort and moderation, for the sake of relativity and balance, but addictions and convictions of the soul are painful to starve.

Chapter 9: Miracle of Music

It was Munich. It was The Odyssey. Beathan was drinking stouts. Kyle was smoking bud. Eric was trying to gain some sympathy for the immense crowd of hippies, and Todd was seeing live music for the first time. Jesus stood in the back, brow scrunched in mild scrutiny when the band walked out. Patrick Carney, drummer of The Black Keys, Brittany Howard, singer and guitarist of Alabama Shakes, Jerry Garcia, singer and guitarist of the Grateful Dead, Bootsy Collins, bassist of Parliament Funkadelic, and singers Grace Potter and Allison Krause formed the blues-funk jam-band, The Odyssey. Bootsy Collins did an instrument check then Jerry Garcia addressed the crowd.

"How ya'll doin' tonight?" Jerry reached out with some feeling in his voice.

The crowd replied with screams of delight. Most of them looked like Kyle with a few exceptions. There were those wearing 'Life is Good' shirts and tie-die, and there were those who looked like gypsies and pirates. It was mayhem, but Christ saw something in these people that Todd couldn't. They sacrificed material wants for something higher, good vibrations. Those vibrations weren't holy or righteous, but the effect they had on the listener were. Between the psychedelic drugs and the music, the hearts stayed warm, but the soul lost direction as the counterculture passed through the 1960's and continued through time into the age of technology and materialism. Peace, love, and understanding wasn't something that was consumed, and Christ came to help these hippies identify that. It wasn't about what went into their bodies, but what came out. Peace, love, and understanding, were soulful and righteous, and if The Odyssey was a catalyst to Christ's teachings, he was determined to remind the world there was not only passion, but ensoulment and eternal salvation.

"What's with all the gypsy and pirate types?" Eric questioned without much sympathy for the crowd.

"Ramblers, the lot of them," Jesus replied.

Beathan just shook his head as a pair of thirtysomethings were doing lines of MDMA next to him. It was a little lusty and artistic for the huntsman.

"It's not all bad. Plenty of humanitarians and philanthropists out their digging these vibes, J.C." Kyle said to Jesus in jest.

"It's a hard road they'll walk because of it." The Lord's words steered Kyle to where he needed to be. The ecstasy was tempting, but the the spirit of Christ there with him was more fulfilling.

"Whatever happened to being in it for the music?" Eric squeaked.

"The music gets you high. The drugs get you higher," Beathan replied.

The band had started, and they were picking up steam. Bootsy Collins and Patrick Carney were leading the direction of the tunes. The rhythm section was funky, explosive, and staggering. Brittney Howard and Jerry Garcia were spilling soulful blues on guitar at a tempo that matched the rhythm. Grace Potter and Allison Krause were singing with angelic voices. The music crawled and bopped along. The lights caught glaring images of the band. They looked anything but human. Power, rhythm, and ecstasy brewed from the band and flowed out over the crowd. The vibrations emulsified into a groovy soup, thick and pungent with blues, folk, and funk. Primal impulses shot through the spine and head as beastly tones emanated from each musician. Brains were vaporized into ether, and smoke rolled out of the ears of the crowd. Supernatural forces filled the soul of each bandmate. Jerry Garcia's beard looked like a mat of vines. His guitar cried notes that were otherworldly with high pitch and vibrato. Grace Potter and Allison Krause glowed and fluttered about like nymphs on the stage. The beauty in their voices was match with an angelic appearance, crisp, clean, and gorgeous. Bootsy Collins looked like a dragon slapping his bass fast and loose. The funky, low notes never stopped coming. It was sonic overload. He grabbed a gear and downshifted into a bebop mayhem. Patrick Carney looked like a monstrous troll at the back of the stage pounding the tubs and skins, a pure savage. It culminated into something so incredible that the crowd couldn't tell what was taking them higher, the drugs or the music. Brittany Howard wailed over the drums and bass, as Jerry shredded on guitar. The vibrations drove deep into the central nervous system, irie, fresh, and heavy. The music felt like a groovy bender of audial intoxication. It was a harmonic experience of concentrated energy and collective consciousness. The fans bobbed and danced about with the music, and Todd was beginning to see how alive The Odyssey could make a person feel. For some it was the definition of getting spiritual. The Lord was feeling the *music*, but the band's shape shifting was without a doubt an attention getter. Jesus just kept an eye on the crowd. Through their squinted eyes, most wore twinkling smiles on their faces.

"With a band like this, who needs drugs?" Jesus asked his disciples, a little excited himself.

Was it spiritual, or just psychedelic? When the band was done playing, Jesus and his four disciples left the venue and made their way back to Aunt Frieda's cottage.

"Could you get any higher!" Kyle expressed to the other four guys as they walked.

"Kyle, you're beginning to see what I mean by incredible worship," Christ replied.

"Lord, I mean on this planet. We *were* on this planet the whole time, right?" Jesus just laughed at Kyle.

"There were a lot of people having a good time. That was a good place, but there is better."

"I know, eternal salvation, but what about living it up?" Kyle remarked.

"Just keep the jams righteous. Getting stoned isn't righteousness, no matter how you crack it."

"What drew you to such a crowd anyway?" Beathan asked.

"They say it's spiritual. I wanted to see."

Chapter 10: An Argument in the Kitchen

The coffee was strong out of the French Press the next morning. Freida was in the shower, and the five disciples were stirring in the kitchen. Eric had a few cups.

"A cigarette would be great with this."

"Don't you feel better since you haven't been smoking?" Jesus asked.

"Yeah, I do, but a cigarette would be perfect right now."

In deep Scottish accent, Beathan expressed his opinion.

"There's a time and place for everything, even things of ill fate."

Jesus thought about it. Pleasures had in moderation appeared tame, maybe not harmless, but at least under control. It was the possibility that things can get excessive and out of hand that labeled many things of indifference as bad. A single cigarette was not an act of sin. A cigarette addiction might be sinful though. A cup of coffee was a good thing. Coffee overload was bad. Jitters and anxiety would soon follow, things God did not intend man to deal with. Too often man creates his own problems by ignoring the warning signs. We dive headlong into pleasures for the thrill of the moment, and give no thought to further consequence, like the many who were snorting MDMA last night. Today they would be paying for it, hopeless, empty, uncomfortable. Was the high worth the come-down? There had to be a way achieve music on a spiritual level that didn't involve drugs. Just a high of faith, hope, and love. Peace and understanding.

In the kitchen, Beathan and Todd were having a bit of an argument.

"Why are you so *dismissive* to the Lord?" Todd begged of Beathan.

"What has he done for *me*? I live *my own* life. I solve *my own* problems. Why do I need to worship this man? Why should I worship any man?"

"He died for you. He died for all of us! The living Son of God. Your only salvation!"

Todd's remarks didn't sit well with Beathan. He was speaking to a man who could not see his own brokenness. He was speaking to a man who never learned the gospel. Todd was getting excited, and sounded like a heretic to Beathan, but something in his accusation struck Beathan's integrity.

"I'll die my own death! And with a bit of luck, vanish into the fog of the Highlands."

"You'll die, we all die, but He is the Son of God!"

"God?"

"Yeah, the Creator of those wonderful Highlands, this wonderful Earth."

"Geology created the Highlands, and this Earth seems to be a curse for more and more as time goes on."

"That's because too few believe what Jesus has taught, what he came here to prove. There is a God!"

"Ha!"

"Sorry it's so hard for you to submit to the Great Spirit, the Creator."

In an instant, Beathan turned red with anger.

"You say I don't know the Great Spirit? I've learned more on my excursions and sacred mushroom trips than you would ever be able to grasp!"

"Ahh, but what was the center of it all? What was the symbol for the greatest meaning? It wasn't a man who spread peace, love, and understanding, or you would believe the Lord, and we wouldn't be having this argument right now."

Todd got in the last word, and Beathan was baffled. The words would bother him for a while, brooding over them as they were all he could think about.... the meaning of it all. Symbols. Mankind. Peace, love, and understand. Kyle was sitting on the back porch smoking a joint with his cup of coffee.

"Want a toke?" Kyle offered the Lord, graciously.

"I'm not sure if I'm allowed."

"You're Jesus! Of course, you're allowed."

Jesus chuckled.

"My Father was never quite certain what to think of the wisdom weed. If I got high, I'd probably start performing miracles left and right, then bring on the Rapture."

Kyle laughed.

"Kyle, I like you. You're sensible and faithful. Why doesn't Beathan share the same views as you?"

"He's a hard-ass. He's not just boisterous like most Scots. He has a chip on his shoulder from all the time he spent in the wilderness. He's an archer. A man who lives to kill, and probably too many mushrooms. Real Scotsmen find balls by singing at church. Beathan tries to find it in what the Druids taught."

"The Druids taught witchcraft, or at least mysticism with a blind eye to the living God. Human sacrifice wasn't out of their league either."

"That could explain a lot. For him, seeing is believing, and sometimes hallucinating is believing. I doubt he ever felt a real connection with anything divine, just primal."

Jesus was determined to persuade Beathan to believe. He just needed the man to connect, feel something, some kind of proof. Like Beathan, too many believed in a higher power, but it was something remote from humanity. It seemed to be animistic to the millions of agnostic souls on this planet. Why should God have a son? A daughter? Because, he has billions of them, and none too lowly for his love. Some think too lowly of themselves to accept God's love. Some think so highly of themselves that they deny needing forgiveness and salvation. It's not completely the person's fault, but the fault of people, or society. Damning acts were carried out by the clergy, and in the name of the church throughout history, such that anything Christian carried a stigma to the common man in modern times. As the common man tried to distance himself from a "bad religion," the truth and teachings of Christ were forgotten and silenced. Society advanced conceptually and materialistically, and people began developing an outlook that morals were separate from faith in a Living God, despite the righteousness that that Living God carries. They forgot their inherent brokenness and the need for salvation. The common man tried to transcend above the institution of the church and live compassionate lives without faith. The self- saving directive of humanitarians, though noble, had become more highly regarded than having a relationship with God and Christ. That's what Jesus came back to change. To show people that the message taught for centuries was estranged from the truth, and with the help of The Odyssey, the counterculture would come to know the prodigal God.

    Beathan and Kyle packed their bags, and the rest of the crew put their shoes on. They were off to the train station ready to catch another night with the Odyssey. The next show was in Poland, and the train ride to Warsaw would take about two days. It was around noon when the five guys boarded. They walked to their seats in coach and sat down. There was a lull about them through the afternoon as they watched the Bavarian countryside pass by. Todd, Eric, Kyle, and Beathan felt like travelers. There was no appointment to be met. There was no urgency in their journey. Just discretion in time and space. Thoughts evolved in the mind as the land passed by on the other side of the window, and each man had his own ideas about life. Each of them wondered exactly what was the purpose of creation? The self? The crowd? The environment? Or how they all flowed together in unity to perpetuate the good and make the most of things?

Chapter 11: Peace Be with You

The train pulled into Warsaw in the middle of the night. There was soft glee glowing in the darkness. The people of Poland were warm and welcoming. Jesus felt at home. Righteousness was coupled with sincerity. The spirit was with them. The men were not tired despite the hour.

"Sir, you dropped your wallet," a stranger addressed Beathan.

The words were in Polish, but Beathan understood every bit of what the man said. A look of confusion ran over his face. He expected the stranger to take off with the money and credit cards, but instead, the stranger came to the aid of the Bavarian Druid. Beathan flipped through his wallet to make sure everything was there. It was.

"Thanks," Beathan obliged with a bit of confusion.

As Jesus and his disciples made their way out of the train station, something could be sensed that there was much more to these people's lives than the size of their bank accounts. There was a great deal of care for the next person that could be seen, and felt. It was rich and frothy, full bodied like a pint of imperial stout. A sense of welcome, even hospitality, were about them. They carried the faith to please those around them. They wanted everyone to feel loved and accepted, that is, if everyone could reciprocate those feelings. It was done with gentle encouragement, honesty, and savory food. The train station was different than just a hub of travel. It was a place where good vibes could be felt as people passed. People were coming and going and carrying the spirit of hospitality and comfort with them. The ability to provide pleasure and comfort wasn't a materialistic focus. It was more visceral than that. Hard work, patience, and temperance provided *at least* as much delight for the Polish people as money could. Poland was not at the top of the economic food chain, but its people found ways to be happy nonetheless. In the past few decades, the economy had been growing, but their true wealth was spirit. Their richness was drawn from faith. They loved their neighbors as they loved themselves. They were mostly Christian. It wasn't a sense of pride, but an ideal of trust that Christ's teachings would deliver a life of joy and peace. God had blessed the faithful despite the troubles they faced in the Second World War. Maybe they might not have been the most comfortable of people, but in some ways they were. They succeeded in food, drink, and intimacy with great magnitude. Seek and ye shall find. That seemed to be the mantra of the Polish people. They sought love and righteousness, and their hearts were blessed with economic progress. Through their faith and love, they were moving out of depression, tyranny, and squalor.

    Todd and Kyle could feel the embrace of Poland and its people. The other two weren't numb to the love, but it was alien to them. They didn't know how to embrace it. Eric felt so disheveled for so long that connecting with love was awkward. It felt unnatural and uncomfortable. How could total strangers care who you were and how you felt? Beathan thought the same thing, but Beathan was a bit more cynical about his judgement. He imagined there was a catch to it. Faith and the goodness of love couldn't be enough to motivate a people to encourage, comfort, and validate total strangers with consistency.

    "Let's go for a beer," Eric said. The words caught the other four guys off guard. They didn't expect it from Eric. The love in the air was ebbing Eric to explore the sensation. The atmosphere had him slowly easing out of hopelessness. The good faith he was feeling from the Polish people was spilling over and filling his emptiness.

"Okay," Jesus said, as all eyes were on him.

Jesus and his disciples walked the streets of Warsaw looking for a bar that fit their appetite. After passing a few upscale places, they found Zloto's on the crux between the rich and the poor. Zloto's was a cozy little tavern that had a mixed crowd of young and old, mostly blue-collar types. Folk music with a bluesy, smooth-jazz feel was playing on the juke box when they walked in the dimly lit tavern. The chatter was soft and slow, but laughter interrupted the Slavic conversations.

"Stock." Kyle, Beathan, and Eric asked for pints of lager in Polish tongue.

"Kawa." Jesus and Todd settled on coffee.

They took their drinks and eased into somber jubilation while getting looks that let them know they were the exotics in the joint. Kyle started telling stories about nights in Spain, and the four disciples joked and jostled back and forth. Even Todd who was often deep and serious was loosening up. Jesus just peered at the bar-crowd through pursed eyes interested in the love and kindness that was flowing between friends and neighbors. At the corner of the bar Jesus saw two men discussing something with seriousness.

"I can't," Mieszko said to Lech. "It's too much. I'll find a way," refusing as his friend kept trying to give him money.

"You need your water heater. Do you want to face the challenges like the old days of cold baths and boiling your water?"

"No, but a thousand zloty is too much to take from a friend."

"Don't fear that I will be without because of this gift. I am never without, because I have love. When you love, you have no fear."

"You are generous, Lech. Bless you!"

Lech was fearless with his giving. He knew God would provide for him because of his generosity. It was care for those they loved that built such a society of warmth and comfort. A society delivered from ruin because of the practice of what was preached. The Lord blesses those who are charitable, those who have and give to those who have-not.

All five of them heard what went down, to some degree.

"How much is 1,000 zloty in American currency?" Eric asked.

"About $300," Beathan replied.

The men quietly finished their drinks. $300 wasn't an unheard amount to give, but it was rare. It was a gift from the heart. Charity defeated the fear, the opposition of love. Lech was fearless and love-filled when he gave Mieszko the 1000 zloty. He knew he had faith that God would take care of whatever needs he had because of his generosity. Lech was not a rich man, but a wise one. He knew how to stretch a dollar and save what money he earned. He didn't squander his wealth. Beathan was baffled. The care between Lech and Mieszko went against his concept of reality, "survival of the fittest." And, it was not machismo, alpha embracing alpha. It was care. It was humanitarian. The ebb and flow of mystical winds failed to glorify any greatness between such a righteous extension of love.

With drinks down, and positive impressions laid deep into their hearts, the cohort of five walked Warsaw in the dark summer night. The air was balmy as it wrapped itself around the souls of Kyle, Beathan, Eric, and Todd. They began to get sleepy.

"Maybe we should find a hostel," Kyle suggested.

"Suppose we walk?" Jesus argued.

No one questioned him. They sensed he was looking for something, but they weren't exactly sure what that was. Beathan dragged his heavy feet, and Kyle rubbed his eyes, trying to stay awake. Eric was getting lost in the good vibrations, and the coffee and the company had Todd in a good mood. They all could tell Jesus hadn't found what he had set out for. No one asked what it was, whether it was a night on the streets, or a warm bed to sleep in. They just kept trudging along, and let the Holy Spirit guide them. Wandering down alleys and posting at cross walks, there were dozens of impressions left in the mind. But, none held the significance Jesus was looking for in the Warsaw night, until they stumbled upon a quaint overgrown park near the outskirts of the city. Kyle and Beathan sprawled out on the grass with their packs tucked under their heads like pillows. Eric and Todd sat on either side of Jesus and nodded off to sleep. The air was dark and still, yet comforting. A blind man gently tapped his cane on the ground as morning twilight waxed in. Jesus's heart bled for the man. Christ stood up and walked towards the man.

"Fellow, what is your name?"

Jesus' voice was as soft and innocent as a lamb. The blind man eased at the sound of it.

"Aron. Why?"

Jesus brushed his fingertips over the man's eyelids. Something stirred in the air. Strength and beauty seemed to gust, and a queer sensation of consciousness carried through the soul and the atmosphere.

"Aron, open your eyes."

Aron opened his eyes with a bit of shock. He was seeing the sunrise for the first time in his life. After 60 years of living, the beautiful sight of a dawning day filled him with more joy than he could hold in. The man welled up with tears. He saw the world with the unpolluted perception of a child. Life now felt sweeter than ever by the grace of God. Jesus sat back down on the bench, fully knowing Aron's gratitude. Eric saw what happened, but the other three men remained asleep. He was in awe himself, and better understood the gifts of God's grace.

Chapter 12: River Souls and Desert Bandits

About the time The Odyssey got things kicking off in Warsaw, Nick and Rafa were landing in Iran ready to paddle the Sezar River, another class V, world renowned run. As they ventured into the mountains to chase whitewater, they felt uncomfortable. They were outsiders, and unwelcomed at that. In all the other places they ventured to go paddling, they were welcomed with warmth and curiosity. This was different. There was a culture clash. Nick and Rafa represented something pure and innocent. It wasn't an idea of theology that put these paddlers in Iran, but a few couldn't see past their culture and religion enough to embrace, or at least accept, what passion brought these two paddlers to the Zagros Mountains. The energy of this place gave Nick and Rafa premonitions that something bad was about to happen to them. Bandits from the Arabia Desert were chasing vibes, trying to defeat anything that appeared to *sustain* the good. Kayaking and whitewater-culture were of these things. Their energy was free and peaceful, a communion with nature where the spirit was found. Word got out that two American river-hippies were chasing bomb flow in the land of Ismael and Muhamad. The aura about Nick and Rafa caught the attention of the Arabian Bandits, and enraged them. Free-spirited thrill seekers challenged the culture more than the theology of the region, but the ideology and mannerisms of the paddlers were something completely unrelatable and alien to the Arabian Bandits. Their aura expressed the power-of-will to be stronger than fate. Insight to the soul, will, and the passion of the paddlers were ignored as the impulse to defeat the tranquil, rolling vibes of the paddlers ran through the bandits.

Nick and Rafa were going down jeep trails in the Zagros Mountains in their outdated SUV with boats on the roof when they came to a coulee in the topography. As soon as they passed the mouth of the coulee, a convoy of Arabian Bandits stood behind their vehicles with guns drawn. Nick hit the brakes, and tried to slowly creep back in reverse like prey evading its predator. Once the bandits saw the truck moving back, they fired a warning shot, then Nick took off. It was to no avail. There were marauders all over the place dressed in black robes with black turbans firing automatic rifles.

"Fuck it! *This* is bullshit." Nick let on to Rafa who sat beside him in the outdated Land Rover.

Rafa was so bewildered that he broke into laughter.

"What's so funny?" Nick asked.

"Think about it dude, we've been doing this for so long, it was only a matter of time till we got ambushed. They're probably gonna kidnap us."

"And, you're not scared?"

"Were you scared on the Inca? Were you scared on the Zambezi? Just another page in the story. We all die someday. It'd be great to go out in valiant fashion."

Nick didn't lose his nerve, but he shook his head and shut the engine off on the Land Rover. Bandits started walking over to the SUV. They trudged in foot by foot.

"I wish I had a gun," Nick said to Rafa.

"Feel the fire in your soul…"

Taking Rafa's advice, Nick thought of all the raucous swell he had paddled in his life. Then something unexpected happened. Nick transformed into flowing blue liquid while maintaining his muscular form. Rafa did too, but a little more green than that of Nick's. The bandits saw this and started screaming in Arabic. Nick and Rafa stepped out of the Land Rover, and all of Arabian Bandits rushed in with guns pointed and shots firing. Some bullets pierced the water-men but no wounds were inflicted. The bullets just flew through their liquid bodies and plopped out into the sand behind them. The bandits rushed in, hoping to stomp the paddlers to the ground. They overtook Nick and Rafa, but the two paddlers never completely returned to their fleshy-forms.

They were loaded into a truck, and cruised into the coulee where the ambush came from. The truck stopped at the mouth of a cave and Nick and Rafa were forced in.

"Who are you!?" Haziz, the lead bandit, demanded.

"We are *River Souls,*" Nick rebuked with haughty disdain.

"Who!?"

"Sons of the River God."

"God has no sons! It is written, God has no sons!" Haziz and his bandits went on decreeing factions of fate and fertility refusing that their god should have any children, much less sons.

"You must be devils! You shape shift! You must be devils!"

"Uh, no dude, we met Jesus when we got off the Colorado River a few weeks ago and he was cool with us."

"Jesus is a devil!"

"Last time I checked he was the Son of God."

"God shall have no son! These claims are lies!"

Raucous swells of whitewater exploded from Nick and Rafa's bodies. The whitewater was taking its toll on the bandits. Some dropped over dead, some survived heavy blows, and a handful went unscathed. Some of the bandits were intimidated. Others were just angry, and they kept interrogating.

"You met this Jesus?"

"What do you care?"

"He is a false messiah! His teachings ruin us! His followers piss on us!"

Rafa laughed, and Nick just shook his head.

"So, what if we met Jesus?"

"You will take us to him, or we will fill you with sand!"

"Looks like we're going to England," Rafa mumbled.

"Hey, can we get a run in on the Sezar before we go chasin' Jesus?" Nick asked the head bandit with sincerity.

Haziz just put his hands over his face, and screamed.

Chapter 13: Michael Joseph

Michael Joseph was a burly Jew, dark skin, dark wiry hair. He hailed from the mountains of Slovakia, where he worked in timber management. He stood 6 foot 2 inches tall and weighed about 220 pounds. Something in his soul was drawn to the heady grooves of The Odyssey. For over a decade he worked lumberjacking and surveying stands of trees, and frequenting the music of Jerry Garcia and Patrick Carney. It wasn't a vibe that really identified with the integrity of Eastern Europeans, but the tunes matched well with the heady arborists he worked with. Forestry was his family's heritage. Heritage ran deep in his family, as it did for most Eastern Europeans. Forestry wasn't the only factor of heritage for Michael Joseph, religion was as well, Judaism to be exact. Belief in the same god as Christians, but also believing that Christ was not the true messiah, and the real messiah is yet to come. Michael was smoking some cheebah at the show in Warsaw when he made eye-contact with Jesus. He found it a little comical that a longhaired hippy was wearing a white robe in the 21st century. Michael Joseph wasn't there to judge, but there was allure to the man he witnessed. Something drew him to Jesus's acquaintance. Jesus appeared to be observing rather than listening, observing the relationship between the crowd, the band, and the music. Michael Joseph found him a bit peculiar, but the dude looked like he needed a friend. Jesus looked like a man who felt out of place, calm amidst raucous jams. The crowd was energetic, and sang, danced, and cheered with passion. Kyle and Beathan were bobbing and dancing to the music. Eric was snapping his fingers and tapping his foot. Todd wore the same expression as the Lord, attentive and focused. Thick funk, jazz, and blues emulsified in the air. The music sent vibrations into the soul that demanded a reaction of something smooth and hip. The brawny Michael Joseph gazed at the band, and moved in time with the music as he worked his way over to Jesus and his disciples. The grooves were transcending. They were like nothing else on Earth. Michael Joseph could feel the Holy Spirit flow between something in the crowd and the band, as if it were coming out of the man he was now standing next to. Christ smiled, and began nodding his head in time with the music. Michael Joseph shook his head as he heard his consciousness whisper to him, "*He is the Messiah!*" over, and over again. It was unnerving, hearing it as he grooved to the music and smoked his weed. He tried to put the voice out of his head, but it overcame him, forcing him to address it. Michael Joseph took a long toke on his fat doobie and held it out in front of Jesus.

"Christ! Enjoy some man!*"*

Jesus took the joint from the burly Jew, held it to his nose, and smelled the smoke rolling off its cherry.

"Good stuff," Jesus said with a smile, handing the joint back to Michael.

"Go ahead, take a hit! Makes you feel alive."

"But, Michael, I am the life, the truth, and the way," Jesus replied with sincerity. There was significant magnitude in what he had just told Michael Joseph. The words rang true for two thousand years, but in that moment, Michael Joseph had seen, heard, and felt spiritual evidence. It was more gripping than the weed or the music. It was a transcendental high, standing exclusively upon the medium of social communication. Michael took a small drag off his doober, and reflected for a moment. For reasons unexplained, nothing felt as important as knowing the man he was standing next to.

"Come," Jesus said to Michael.

They began walking through the crowd. The Odyssey jammed loud and proud. Love emanated from Jerry's guitar. Bootsy and Patrick punched with funk. Brittany Howard and the girls wailed away, powerfully. The energy excited the passions of the crowd. The jam was getting spiritual on a number of levels as Michael Joseph followed Jesus through the crowd. Everyone was grooving to the heady vibes while Jesus worked miracles to the beat of the Odyssey. Jesus hit the activation energy. The spirit of the music molded and forged the fans into something primal and psychedelic. As Jesus touched people, they changed form into birds, lizards, bears, everything. He bumped up against a righteous sage, and when he touched the man, he turned into a cloud, strobing pink and silver, occasionally striking with lightning. As the music flowed and rippled through time, each fan was struck with a spiritual energy forging the supernatural. The only question was what were they placing their faith in? Music and drugs appeared to be the primary objects of faith. Michael Joseph saw through the fog, and had explicit proof of who and how these miracles were being worked. It was Christ.

Chapter 14: Mayhem

Haziz shook his fist and garbled something in Arabic about Nick and Rafa. Nick pulled a copy of *Canoe and Kayaking Magazine* out from his back pocket and began reading.

"Look here. Arabian Bandits are mad because they live in a place that's *too dry* and they have *too many wives!*"

"Ahgarble garble! Abuhgah hubug!" Haziz went off. "Stirp them of their things!" One Arabian Bandit started ripping the clothes off of Nick and Rafa.

"Don't threaten me with a good time!" Rafa joked.

One man pulled up a gun and pulled the trigger. Rafa put his watery finger in the barrel of the gun, and the back end exploded, blasting the bandit back against the wall of the cave. Nick and Rafa just laughed. They laughed harder and harder, and jets of water sprayed from their groins, pushing all the bandits out of the cave.

"What do we do, boss?" Ahmed asked Haziz.

"Sandbag them!"

Chapter 15: Righteousness

The show was winding down and sweaty hippies were growing tired as they danced to the music and the drugs wore off. Michael Joseph was dancing like a freak. Warsaw was groovin'. The Odyssey left their mark on the town. One more show. One more night on the edge. Bootsy Collins was reelin' in the beats.

"Can you get any higher!?"(Bootsy)

"Man, I felt alive!"(Patrick)

"I think I saw a man turn into perogies!" (Brittany) "What are we jamming on!?"

"Vibrations. Just shedding the vibes" (Jerry) "The Munich Show was hot, but tonight was scorchin.'"

"I saw a guy who looked just like Jesus." (Patrick)

"Yeah there were about a thousand of them." (Jerry)

"All of God's righteous children." (Brittany)

The banter went silent for a minute, then Patrick piped up.

"What makes our work righteous?" he asked with serious curiosity.

"Amplitude," Bootsy replied with a hip grin. Brittany Howard just scratched her head.

"Peace. Love. And Understanding," Jerry rebutted.

"Jerry, the sixties were decades ago." (Patrick)

They all exhaled into a quieter realm, and decompressed after a rather spiritual jam. The word 'righteous' remained in their minds. It had been the adjective of choice for what the music did. But, what did the music really do? The band understood that the music brought people together to witness a colorful expression of soul, but was it love that spread beyond the witness, or was it just good for personal gain? There was a spectrum of worth, spanning from pride and egotism, to love and sharing that was brought on by the music. Jesus was trying to capture the love and sharing, and trying to dissolve the egotism that was attached to witnessing righteous music. He was not only the mark of faith and repentance, but also the mark of the utilitarian good, showing people how to love and put others before yourself. Jesus was sent to a broken race of sinners to die the death we all deserved to die. That was forgotten and had stopped being taught. If Jesus could return to people who spread peace, love, and understanding, maybe the light of truth could fill their soul, and add depth to their spirit. If a spiritual moment developed in the music, hopefully it could benefit the communal good, and it seemed to. Hopefully it was not an end in-and-of itself. The energy that was derived from the jams ebbed the consciousness in profound ways. It seasoned its fans to become the salt of the Earth. That salt should have the knowledge and wisdom to know what it truly meant to "get spiritual." The music was energetic and stimulating. It was gripping, and inspired a following. Jesus wanted these people to hold Him and their music in the same breath. Multitudes of hippies were going unknowingly into atheism at the fault of the culture. It was the evil work of the times, and these peaceful, loving hearts would be damned at judgement if Jesus and His disciples couldn't win them back.

The band had a following that rivaled major religious groups. Fans took great pride in which shows they have 'been part of'. They were completely euphoric experiences. The jam melted hot and flowed out over the crowd, seeping into the souls of the fans, sending them into a surreal experience. That experience is a sacred unification of artist and audience. The band becomes a single entity, delivering dynamic vibrations that reach down into the soul, finding the passion of the audience, creating a single unified body of witness. They were truly transcendental experiences, but without true faith, they left the viewer a little delusional. Cosmic energy and good vibes were confused with Holy Spirit and Divine Intervention. Perspectives and personalities became overwhelming with new-age spirituality that idolized mind expansion and live music. Putting the shows in place of the Almighty, and confusion between love and excitement left the extreme end of the culture just as overwhelming as religious radicals and heretics. Many things have been carried out in the Messiah's name: war, genocide, rape. But, something as righteous as music *could not* be stamped as heathen or atheist. It carried the spirit which could unify people and spread love unlike many other things; literature, ideology, theatre, and drama included. Likewise, those in the delusions of hip-culture and new-age-spiritualism needed to find a little moderation: God with a pinch of dogma.

"Can you turn me into perogies, again?" Michael Joseph asked Christ with a bit of a grin. Without saying a word, Jesus touched Michael Joseph, and he immediately became a giant potato-filled-doughball.

"How do you do that!?" Kyle exclaimed.

"Nevermind the metaphysics. The better question is why. I need you to help fill the void. I see something special in the hip counterculture and need the faith behind me just as hippies need salvation through faith in me."

"What if you gave everyone the power to be perogies? Then they'd believe!"

"There's a thought!"

"I wanna be a mushroom," Beathan demanded.

Jesus turned Beathan into a six-foot-tall mushroom.

Everyone laughed heartily.

"Can I turn you back into the Bavarian Druid you were just a moment ago?"

The mushroom wriggled and nodded.

Beathan came back to himself, breathing heavily.

The battle for righteousness was painstaking. The incredibly beautiful flow between The Odyssey and its audience helped numb the pain. It was a catalyst in the ebb-and-flow of dynamic equilibrium. It was evidence of the Spirit in the here-and-now. That was the same effect Christ wanted to show of Himself. It was tangible-hope to face the challenges of life.

"When war is waged between good and evil, energy and consciousness of the good must outweigh that of evil. Otherwise, there is tyranny and oppressions. Despots and marauders seek to land crushing blows, and if the world grows numb and ignorant to what is Holy and righteous, evil will defeat good. Then, there is no peace."

Chapter 16: Fruit of the Spirit

In Iran, the kayakers were frustrating the Arabian Bandits. Haziz was trying to get a grasp on why these men had the power of raging rivers about their watery frames. It was a matter of righteousness. It was a matter of passion. Steep water and bomb flows lit a fire within the souls of these two men, and it was something so pure and so thrilling that God could not ignore the spirit of Nick or Rafa. No, they were blessed with supernatural power because of the *purity and innocence of their passions*. The bandits had passion of nothing pure or innocent. Brutality and oppression in the name of holiness was no match for what the fruitful naturalists held close to their hearts. Their passions revolved around something that was fruitful and bountiful, not dead and empty. Passions for good things builds strength and character. True passion for good things produces Fruits of the Spirit, which are love, joy, peace, patience, kindness, goodness, faithfulness, gentleness, and self-control. Passions for bad things brings emptiness to the soul. Murder and kidnap were not the message of a righteous man or a righteous messiah. Haziz and his gang were following delusional lies. They had passion for bringing retribution to people who were not even their enemies. They were lords of hate.

The bandits couldn't keep a tight lock on the kayakers. Nick managed to pack a pipe full of Sativa grown in the Himalayas mixed with some Indica from Crete. Nick hit the bowl and passed it to Rafa. Rafa took a hit and the two of them flipped through the kayaking magazine they had with them.

"Why are we holding them captive? They are just a couple of pot-smoking river-hippies," Ahmed asked Haziz.

"This Christ guy… claims to be the son of God… God cannot have a son! God is only fate and fertility!"

"Right… but why them?"

"They are going to take us to Christ!"

"Wanna hit this, man?" Nick offered the bowl to Haziz.

Chapter 17: A Long Strange Trip

Jesus, Michael Joseph, and the rest of the disciples were connecting the dots on their way to Helsinki, Finland. Their trip from Poland to Finland would take them through Lithuania, Latvia, and Estonia. After passing through Estonia, they would take a ferry from Talinn, across the Gulf of Finland, and into Helsinki.

When they made it into Lithuania things got strange. The world felt depressed. There was a darkness that loomed, and everything felt cold. This was the land of the have-not's, a second world country, previously part of the Soviet Union. There was no escape. Winds blew in off the Baltic Sea, far away where the air was fresh, and the people felt free. Tenements and shanties lined the streets, people building shelter with whatever they could find. It was a symbol of what greed and tyranny could do to an entire nation. It appeared as though God turned his back on them. They were not the first of his chosen people, but still these people carried the faith that one day, when they lay their burdens down, and pass on to the next life, there would be no sickness, no toil, no danger. The streets were dirt, and the water unsafe to drink. The devil appeared to have gotten the upper hand. There were not even any great deserts for clans of people to retreat for fasting in search of answers. These people lived hand-to-mouth, surviving anyway they could. The communist regime of the Soviets destroyed wealth, health, and happiness for many societies, Lithuania being just one of those brought to ruin. Still many symbols of Christianity could be seen as Jesus and his disciples passed through. Jesus made sure not to take the train all the way through the Baltic States enroute to Finland. He wanted show the boys something.

"These were some of the last people of the western world to be taught the gospel. They were last in line. There will be a day when the last shall be first, and the first shall be last."

The world may have forgotten about them, but Christ did not. Jesus Christ, Lord and Savior, fed their soul and spirit. When they had nothing else to sustain them, Christ gave them hope. The presence of God's Spirit brought them peace and comfort in ways that luxury and convenience could not. He was the fuel that drove their spirits forward day after day when they had nothing else to look forward to. Faith gave them something intangible, something that was strong and steadfast. Something no one could take away. Something that helped them find beauty in the little things when there was nothing else to be had.

"The wealth of those who ruled these once-pagan-people fueled the flames of oppression. These Eastern Slavs were viewed as property. They were lower than slaves. Now their world was trying to catch up for lost time… I don't know if they will ever see grand lives like those lived by those in first-world countries. They may go on in squalor until rapture. But they have more passion about eternal salvation than those who have been given royalty, or even just a comfortable life. What they want is not an economic commodity. It cannot be bought and sold in the marketplace. It's that yearning for something promised through the spirit and the soul, something that glimmers through the darkness in bits and pieces with just enough brilliance to hold truth. Some people never see that brilliance, but these are not some of those people."

Winds blew in from the northwest off the Baltic Sea far away. It could not be seen, but its presence could be felt. It was ether that filled the lungs and sinuses with divine stimulation. The energy had spirit, a sense of consciousness that ebbed and flowed in the mind causing the self to flow with the tides, breathing hope of a bountiful life, in this world and the next. It sustained a passion that something magical existed in the great beyond. It was faith in promises of things unseen. It was righteous far beyond any concert, but seeing The Odyssey was something like that ethereal breeze. It breathed life into the listener. The vibrations were divine stimulation. If only the audience of The Odyssey had the same steadfast faith in the Great Creator and his Son as the Lithuanians did. There were a lot of similarities between the vibes of The Odyssey and the Baltic breeze. It was energy and habit, or consciousness, if you will. It was spiritual. The passion of feeling salvation was all encompassing, but just where that salvation came from was the difference between the fans of The Odyssey and the Christian faithful. Most Lithuanians never heard the music from Jerry Garcia, but that is not to say they never heard the most beautiful vibrations and most beautiful message. *The way, the truth, and the life* were laid before these people of poor economic standing, and they grasped God's righteousness tightly. It was transcending and supernatural. It broke the bounds of our world and soared into the great beyond. What The Odyssey had was primal and visceral. Even a spiritual experience by The Odyssey could not match the eternal hope and Holy Promise of Christ. Christ didn't make you pay an admission. He simply requested that you believe in Him. It was intentionally an easy bargain for man, for God wants to invite us into His kingdom.

Jesus and his disciples made it out of the poorer regions of Lithuania, and worked their way towards the coast. The air was brisk and sobering, blowing in from the brilliant purple skies above the sea. The sand beneath their feet was hard, giving way just a little as they took step after step. The atmosphere was taking Beathan back to somewhere he could relate to, the Scottish Highlands. It wasn't a misty mountaintop, but the environment was softening his pride and coaxing his soul towards divinity. After seeing the peace that Christ delivered to the people of Eastern Europe, the long walk down the beach of the Baltic Sea harmonized the natural essences of the Spirit with the humanitarian-strength of Christianity.

Todd walked beside Beathan, and they shared a moment of clarity. It wasn't the hard work of each step up a mountain or the adrenaline of closing in on an animal that Beathan was feeling. What he was feeling was more like a cup of coffee at sunrise, a revelation of hope. Determination was not the vehicle that carried the moment. Comfort was found in perspective; what they were viewing and how they looked at it. With a view base in Christian faith, nature appeared as an extension of the human race. It was built by the Creator to facilitate love and wisdom between all people and this great Earth. There was comfort in the faith of a supernatural force that watched over us and all this land. Beathan was beginning to see true divinity. Todd had been seeing it all along, but he hadn't taken his meds in awhile. The symptoms were beginning to show.

"You okay?" Jesus asked. "You look about as disheveled as Eric did back in Santa Barbara. You keep talking in circles too quietly for anyone to hear."

Michael Joseph felt a stirring in his soul. Belief in Christ was stronger than the magnetism he felt at the show in Warsaw. It burned with a fire that desired proclamation of his love and faith.

"Christ, I now know you as Messiah… Would you baptize me so that I may confess you as my savior?" he asked.

"Come," Jesus said.

The two walked out into the sea to where the waves rolled in at waist-height.

Jesus stood behind Michael.

"Do you reject Satan? And all his works? And all his empty promises?" Jesus asked.

"I do," Michael Joseph replied.

Jesus dunked Michael Joseph once.

"Do you believe in God, the Father, Almighty Creator of heaven and earth? Do you believe in Jesus Christ, his only Son, our Lord, who was born of the Virgin Mary, was crucified, died, and was buried, rose from the dead, and is now standing here with you?"

"I do."

Jesus dunked Michael a second time.

"Do you believe in the Holy Spirit, the church of God, the communion of saints, the forgiveness of sins, the resurrection of the body, and life everlasting?"

"I do," Michael Joseph replied.

Jesus dunked Michael a third time. When Michael Joseph rose out of the water, Jesus said these words.

"God, the all-powerful Father of Christ, has given new you birth by water and the Holy Spirit, and has forgiven all your sins. Go forth with faith in me forever and ever."

The six of them walked north down the beach in the late hours of evening twilight. Michael Joseph was a step or two ahead of the rest of the clan. He was filled with new life. Truth flowed within and around him, as he walked on with new faith and direction. He was awakened and determined to live a faithful Christian life. Eric, too, was taken away. For the first time since his acid trip months ago, he felt whole. The Holy spirit flowed from the Heavens, through the coast, and into his soul. He found peace and fulfillment on the Baltic coast in the presence of the Lord. He had nothing, except for faith. "A Jew was just baptized by Christ!" Eric thought. The spirit was flowing with strength through these six men. The lust in Kyle, the mania in Todd, the emptiness in Eric, and the pride within Beathan dissolved with Michael Joseph's conversion to Christianity. With Christ, these five men felt as though there was nothing they could not accomplish. The Spirit was with them, and they felt bold and righteous. The world was changing. But, for all the good that came about, there was an equal measure of evil brewing. Christ needed his warriors. He needed peace makers, strong, charitable souls. Spite and envy were spreading through the world. Christ needed a new wave of faithful as much as pagan hippies needed salvation through Him. Nick and Rafa were trapped by haters seeking to stop the connection between love and faith. A radical new tyrant was raining oppression on free spirits just as the Soviets had tyrannized the Slavic people for centuries. Tyranny and oppression were nothing new. It feasted on the weak, humble, and unsuspecting. It was fueled by greed for money and power. What the tyrants fail to accept is that knowledge is power, and the ability to communicate knowledge is power. Christ was working to deliver the knowledge of salvation to those souls unsuspecting the tyranny of the Arabian Bandits. For all the wars fought, good was pitted against evil. Over the years, evil had been absolved, and was beginning to seem harmless. And good was beginning to seem useless. It was this bit of ignorance that Christ came to expose, and defeat. He had been mighty in battle against evil things in his mortal life, and was still mighty in his return. Through him, his disciples found strength, and hope, and power.

Once they got to Latvia, Jesus and his five disciples boarded a train to Talinn. Todd's habits were becoming overwhelming. He was beginning to hallucinate, seeing light and shadows break before him. He took them as signs of good and evil, and recited scripture trying to protect himself and those around him from evil forces. Beathan didn't know what to do about it, but he couldn't handle Todd anymore. He snuck off to the café car to have a beer in solitude. Beathan sat alone in thought for a few minutes. "Do I need them? Do they need me? I don't even think I'm enjoying this anymore." Beathan continued to ponder the purpose of the whole trip, and what was in it for him. Then Jesus walked up to him with a beer of his own in hand.

"May I sit with you?"

Beathan gestured for the Lord to take a seat. The two of them sipped their beers in peace and quiet. When Jesus finished his, he left Beathan by himself with even more to think about. "What could be gained from this whole thing? What did it mean to be Christian? Was it a sign of weakness?" At one time he may have thought that. He may have thought that it was braver to have faith in one's self than to submit to a higher power, but after seeing the way Todd carried himself in the fear of schizophrenia, Beathan thought deeper about what it meant to have strength and be spiritual. The delusions that surfaced from his mushroom-trip vision-quests paralleled Todd's psychosis. But from an internal, first-person perspective, they appeared to be the truth. What

Beathan believed to be the truth was changing the longer the trip went on. As much he hated to admit it, he was gaining faith. It was an epiphany that hearkened the soul to a brilliant world that was previously left in the dark. It's admitting that you are broken and being honest with yourself. As you do, the most fundamental purposes of life and humanity develop into passions. The dry rot of disbelief fails, and becomes filled with the faith that there is more to life than what is present at face value. There is more to life than what we see here on Earth. Want changes from desires of riches and wealth, to that of the higher pleasures; keeping the peace, spreading health and happiness, having faith that the soul is saved after death. When Beathan sat with Jesus in that café car he felt something different from the usual familiarity of grit and brawn. There was comfort on those quiet moments. For some reason Beathan felt that he knew where he was going. His back wasn't against the wall but his face wasn't peering into the strange void of futility. In that moment, he felt as though living for personal gain was pointless. There were no prospects to admire through mystical insight, and personal strength. The oneness with the natural world that he so pursued was felt as he had a beer with Jesus. It felt like truth, an ebbing and flowing truth that demanded a response, accepting his brokenness, calling upon a savior, and finding harmony with the world through Christ, the Holy Spirit, and God.

    They made it to the show in Helsinki after a long walk up the Baltic Coast to Talinn, and crossing the sea from Estonia to Finland. Brazen from deep thoughts and a long journey, the six men walked into Aleksanterin Teattari. The theatre was dark. The crowd was hip, but far from Holy. Everyone was kind of still for a rock 'n' roll show. Jesus and his five friends were stiff, and somber until Kyle pulled out a joint.

He started puffing on it then passed it over to Jesus. He took a little whiff of the glowing cherry, and that was enough to get him as high as a kite. He reached out, and touched Beathan. Beathan turned into a phosphorescent red deer with brilliant glimmering antlers. Then he reached out to Michael Joseph who turned into a nine-foot-tall forest-troll, hairy and brutish. Kyle shrieked "Hallelujah," and danced with a supernatural breeze blowing his hair back.

The band heard the commotion, and came onstage a few minutes early to see what the fuss was about. Todd and Eric put Christ on their shoulders and started crowd surfing the Lord up to the stage, and Bootsy Collins started slappin' the bass fast and loose. Jerry Garcia played an intro that was way up on the neck of his guitar with a tempo that could have fit into many-a folk song. Patrick Carney was poundin' the tubs and skins with a primal rhythm. The music didn't mesh at first, then it all flowed into something harmonious; euphoric vibrations that sent the soul soaring. Beathan up-and-galloped-off. He was running like an antelope, out of control. Cluster flies glowed overhead, and the crowd was bouncing 'round the room. The Odyssey was grooving with thick freakness. They played slow and dark in minor scales, and hot and fast in majors.

"Keep me clean

Keep me warm

Keep my soul away from harm," Jerry sang.

Sound and color where flying, taking off and coalescing in the atmosphere. Brittany Howard wailed away:

"Keep the night

Keep the day

Keep the in-between away."

The walls shook as Michael Joseph danced with his heavy feet. Jesus crowd surfed all the way up to the stage. In his long hair and white robe, he gave the peace sign to the audience, folded his hands, bowed his head, and moonwalked out over the heads of the crowd. He descended to the floor after covering a few yards, and the whole audience turned into trolls and fairies. Rumors were going around that there was some good acid in Helsinki, but Jesus and his disciples knew better; it was miracles of the Holy Spirit that sent Alexander Theater spinning with magic. The night went on with a supernatural thump-and-glow for hours. Sweat-soaked and alive, the crowd in Helsinki danced until the band simply said "Goodnight!" and walked away.

The next morning Jesus and his five friends found themselves outside of Kahvi Hautua coffee shop sipping java. Beathan was unusually up-beat and talkative. Eric still wore some shades of the nymph he was the night before. Kyle and Todd just grinned and breathed deeply.

"Are you feeling good, Michael Joseph?" Jesus asked.

Michael made no reply. He was a little withdrawn from being a woods troll the night before.

"I've always said it, acting like that really takes it out of a man. A man shouldn't need much rest after recreation."

A beautiful, blonde-haired, Scandinavian girl adjacent to them chuckled.

"Good morning!" Todd greeted the young woman.

She rolled her eyes at him, and went back to her cell phone.

"What might your name be?" Kyle asked with couth.

"Helaina," she replied with supercilious sass. "I take it all of you were at Aleksanterin Teattari last night?" She asked before taking a sip of her kahvi.

"Oh yeah!" Todd, Eric, Kyle, and Beathan replied in unison. Then Todd went on a bit further. "That's Jesus!" Todd exclaimed, pointing at the Lord.

Helaina laughed a bit more, and rolled her eyes.

"Mhmm."

"I guess you had to see the miracles at the show to believe such a thing," Kyle went on.

"Miracles? It sounds more like witchcraft by what I heard." Helaina cracked.

"No, just magical!" Beathan rebutted.

Then all eyes were on Christ.

"Mayhem, is what it was. But I never said being a peacemaker meant maintain the status-quo… Sometimes… it takes drastic measures to get your point across," said Jesus. The Lord had the young lady's attention. "What makes you think I am *not* the Son of God?"

"Pfff."

With a bit of growl in his voice, Todd interjected.

"There is a God. Get over it," Todd interjected with a grin.

"So, is that what the son of God does? Go around performing all these *'miracles'* for hippies to get high on?"

"You should listen more closely. It was a little mayhem to spread a lot of peace."

"So, your Father, The Creator, he made *Adam* and *Eve*, and evolution is just a myth?"

"You are missing the point. The book of Genesis was written to explain how humans strayed from God. Eating from the Tree of Knowledge of Good and Evil was the one thing man was not supposed to do. Because of his disobedience, the entire human race lives in a broken existence, distanced from God. That is not how man was supposed to exist. And now society is hung up on the "how," disputing the mechanics of creation, as if that were important for some reason. Anthropologists say that around the time people made a mass movement out of the garden, early man began eating meat, and the size of the brain transformed through generations, expanding both ability and vice, but that's just what anthropologists believe. What does it mean to *evolve*? Do you really think my Father, with his plans and all-powerful ways, created a world that was static and wouldn't ever change?"

Christ had Helaina's jaw on the ground. The clan laughed, then Michael Joseph let out a terrible grunt. It took everyone by surprise. Michael shook his head and shivered a bit.

"Wiiild..." was the only word that came out of his mouth.

A short moment passed in awkward discomfort. The sunlight shining on Finland intensified, and cried an ethereal song that could barely be heard.

"I feel unclean… I think I should fast..." said Jesus, bringing reverence to the moment, influencing reflection and coaxing contemplation of what was to come.

Chapter 18: Righteous Fasting

    The long hours of high-latitude daylight marked the beginning of Jesus's early summer fast. He thought it might reveal something, something necessary. When the eyes and ears are cleansed, the mind functions with pure cognition. Power is fed by the soul, and righteousness becomes a passion. Vision is keen, and attention is paid to things sacred. The late evening sun of the Helsinki-summer felt eternal. It felt like the ever-burning light at the end of the tunnel. The clan was strutting-about after the show at Alexander Theater, but Christ knew that was not the sole purpose of faith. They saw incredible things, but it wasn't the prime of righteousness, although primal it was. It was an exercise in supernatural peace-keeping. All the whims of the Great Spirit were ebbing and flowing around the Lord, and those closest to him were beginning to feel a change. It wasn't anything they could decisively describe, but they felt different. An unspoken change in direction was about them. Keen insight was within them. They weren't sure where-from, nor why things were changing, but their passions began to blend together into a common focus. Still, they had their questions. What? How? And where next?

    In the few hours of darkness on that high latitude summer night, they made it across the Baltic Sea, back into Estonia. There, natural beauty was matched with simple living. The old ways were not forgotten. The simplicity that brought peace and happiness was embraced, but there was still turmoil. Archaic sects of Judaism matched the numbers of Orthodox Christians. Peace wasn't a homogenous mixture in the land. There was much dispute among people with different beliefs as they lived next to one another. The concept of the great beyond, and truth, and mysticism were quarreled over. 'The right way' was something passed down from generation to generation. Revelation and revolution were often met with objection and disbelief. The ways that worked were proven through experience, but the world was changing faster than ever. Not only did the sayer of salvation need to be brought to the forefront, but the evolving world needed to regain sight of what sacrifice and discipline meant. Generations had strayed from the truth, and there would be a reckoning if they did not regain *the way*.

As they connected train stops with foot-travel, Jesus was overcome with keen focus. He appeared almost mean. He said few words, and rhythmically put one foot in front of the other as they made their way from train station to train station. Some of the clan addressed him with questions and comments about the world they were in, but he didn't have much response until Michael Joseph asked this somewhere near the Belarus-Ukrainian border.

"Lord, what is it that God expects out of us?"

The indigo night was bedazzled with specs of starlight over the sprawling green landscape.

"There are five things. First is to worship. Pray and sign praise. Rejoice for what the Father has given. Appreciate his gifts and exalt his name. Through Worship, you will grow closer to the Father, Son and Holy Spirit. Second is to fellowship. Man was not meant to be a solitary creature. Gather in the name of God, and share in the delight of his wisdom. Congregate with righteous passion. Be a vassal of love and encouragement. It is through fellowship that we validate ourselves. We see how our fellow man may thrive and flourish, and how it applies with the ways we live. It is through fellowship that God can see the embodiment of peace. Third, God watches our discipleship. He sees how we discipline ourselves to become spiritually mature believers. We hone ourselves to become faithful in the Gospel of the Bible. We gain an understanding of theology and wisdom as we make the sacrifices in bettering ourselves as well as bringing others closer to God. Fourth is ministry, carrying forth my mission to the world. Spread peace, love, and understanding through faith in me as your savior. Spread the good news, and give validation to those who seek me. and repent of their sins. Fifth is Evangelism. Testify to the love, joy, and abundance that faithful living has brought you. Spread the Good News that all who live a life of faith in me and repentance of sins shall not perish, but have everlasting life."

The five disciples were calm. There was peace in the air. They thought about what had just been said. Fellowship, worship, discipleship, ministry, and evangelism. Were they doing their part? If not, why would God love them? The answer laid in God's grace and unfailing love. No act we perform could earn us salvation. It is only by God's grace and faith in Christ that we gain salvation. Accepting that we are not holy in our own ways is hard for anyone to swallow. We are a broken race of misanthropes, sinful and distant from God. Our relationship with Him can only be found through Christ. There, we find the face of unfailing love, and see hope that restores us. Todd was most in tune with what God wanted from his children, despite his ways which many considered manic and delusional. He and Michael Joseph were the only ones who worshiped God, at least up until this point, and they were the only ones who pursued spiritual maturity. Kyle and Beathan did their part to fellowship, even if that fellowship wasn't in sacred settings. Eric was questioning himself.

"Where did we go wrong?" he asked Jesus, a bit disheveled.

"For a long period of time, humanity's focus was on growing spiritually, and being faithful. That focus created a world of comfort, just as God promised it would. But people embraced the comfort that faith built instead of pursuing deeper faith. That comfort and the luxury associated with it left people neglecting growth and advancement. They just became happy enough to exist and lost sight of what is to come. A broken race was to be made whole, made new. Evil spread over God's people as they quit practicing their faith. The world became numb and hollow where soul and passion once existed."

Eric was beginning to feel a little ashamed. He looked at the five men he was with. He had not lived the lives they had lived. He did not always believe what they have believed. But he was on a journey. Life was new. Eric was feeling the spirit. The spirit has a way of transcending from soul to soul. Kyle's smooth delight and Todd's devout faith were spilling over onto Eric. He was seeing the light. It was promising. He looked at Beathan who had his head bowed and hands folded. He was praying. It wasn't something he had ever done before.

"Lord Jesus, I want the gift of eternal life. I am a sinner, and have been trusting myself. Right now, I renounce my confidence in myself and put my trust in you. I accept you as my personal savior. I believe you died for my sins, and I want you to come into my life and save me. I want you to be the Lord and Master of my life. Help me turn from my ways and follow you. I am not worthy, but I thank you Lord for saving me. Amen."

He wasn't sure if he did it right, but that didn't matter. Who was to say one form of worship was better than another? Beathan was praying and worshiping in the right way. Eric duplicated what he was seeing. He asked God for forgiveness of the things he was proud of, the things that were not his works and were not for the betterment of the self or mankind. He asked for forgiveness of his luscious and materialistic ways. He needed strength and direction, and the only place he could turn to for those things was God. His eyes were now open.

"Where's the next show? I mean I know were headed south, but no one said where The Odyssey is playing next," Kyle asked.

"Istanbul," Jesus replied.

"You mean Turkey?" Kyle asked again, a bit baffled.

The six men had a long way to go, through Ukraine, then across Romania and Bulgaria.

Chapter 19: Delusional Thinking

They made it to Rivne, Ukraine after 4 days of walking down the E40 highway in northwest Ukraine. Majestic mountains rose from the landscape. And, at the foothills, grassland buffered the bluffs at the bottom of the slopes. The men were exhausted when they reached Rivne, all of them except for Jesus.

"I need to rest," Todd said. "If I keep pushing on, mania is going to set it."

The crew had been watching him slip into psychosis and delusional thinking for the past few days. Now, in his exhausted state he was foreseeing something about himself that was even worse. The introspective realities he declared were hard truths to face, but Todd didn't want to be the monster he might become, if he hadn't already.

"We could probably find a hostel," Beathan replied with indifference. "We have enough time to stop for the night."

They began the hunt for a roof and a bed. As they walked, metal gates and fences guarded the more affluent properties. Then, they made it into the ghetto. Despite the lack of money supporting the area, the living quarters were not monotypical. Small shacks with overgrown yards were nested in quiet hamlets of the ghetto. In the more urbanized areas, the ghetto was home to run down high-rise apartments. Somewhere in the crux between wealth and ruin laid Blues and Jazz, a high-class Eastern Europe blues bar.

"Let's get a beer!" Beathan interjected as the crew passed. Kyle and Beathan began to unshoulder their packs before hearing an answer. They expected the usual allowance of consumption in the moment.

"Not now, not while I'm fasting," Jesus replied.

Beathan, Kyle, and Michael Joseph looked a little disappointed. They half-expected to get the green light, but they had forgotten that there is a time and place for everything. Truly, drinking a beer was not a sin (although getting drunk is), but this was not a moment for libations and recreation. Jesus had his focus on something bigger, and his men needed reminded of that. Jesus was transcending as he continued his fast. He could not be trapped and molded by any vice within Blues and Jazz. He had to be the forge that molded the artifice, and not become the artifice himself. The guys, too, had to maintain form. Jesus could not afford for those men to succumb to vice through the path that begins with innocent distraction from righteousness. Furthermore, they were running out of money, and needed to pay for tickets into Glastonbury Music Festival in a week or two.

Their packs began to feel heavy. The weight of the journey was unloading on them. Maybe that's what Todd was saying when he talked about mania setting in. Metabolically and psychologically he was cycling, and needed a resting cycle. He was running on fumes just as Jesus was. Unfortunately, Todd was prone to psychosis under those conditions.

Something transcendental happens amidst privation of fuel and nutrients. With good direction, the individual transcends into a state of nirvana. Revelations fall before the eyes. Unfortunately, not every psyche is capable of seeing the truth when they fast. What is found along the journey of transcendence depends on the initial direction. If the sights are set on something holy, the journey through privation and along transcendence embetters the individual. Fasting is a journey and a search for improvement. Not only are you cleansing the body, but you are also cleansing the mind. Jesus was trying to distance himself from the vices that surround the underground music culture. The intoxication, the catalyzing of sex, and to some degree the magic that flew from his hands that night in Alexander Theatre were not the holy mission. He didn't favor the fact that people need to see miracles to believe who he is, and the way of truth that he taught. He hoped it could just be accepted that he was the Messiah. Unfortunately, humans were not perfect creatures. We can be proud and greedy, overlooking the fundamental needs of others. Those needs don't *only* include food, water, and shelter. Being loved and validated is also a fundamental need, a need which has been often overlooked. Love was not shared in Ukraine constantly throughout time; often it was a place of tyranny from the Soviet Union, as well as other regimes through history. Eastern Europe and Central Eurasia were a places of turmoil throughout time. Care and validation were not lavish commodities. Eastern Europe, Mesopotamia, The Soviets, and the Persian empire never seemed to agree on anything. Love was not the care of the government. War was waged over land and religion. The victor often treated the losing culture with tyranny and oppression. It left the soul cold. When Jesus and his disciples made it to the hostel, they could feel the coldness of the country, at least towards strangers. Everyone was suspicious of strangers, outsiders, and the unknown.

  They got two rooms, and slipped off to bed. Jesus was with Beathan and Kyle. Michael Joseph was with Todd and Eric. With lights off and stillness in both bedrooms, Todd meditated. He sat cross legged with hands resting palm-up on his knees. He closed his eyes and sat tall. His head was held at an attentive position, but all he paid attention to was his breathing. Steady breaths filled his lungs. Once they were filled to capacity, he fluidly exhaled, never letting his breathing go still for a moment. After a few minutes of continuous breathing, he started to center his chi. He started to center the focus of his senses. He touched thumb to fingertip, cycling from the pointer to the pinkie and back through. Breath and pulse seemed to control the focus of chi. Once his chi was focused, he relocated its position, moving the focal point of his senses from the top of his head down the chakras of his spine until it fluidly and rhythmically reached the base of his pelvis.

Todd wasn't trying to achieve an out of body experience. No, he was simply trying to reach a sense of peace, equilibrium between mind and body. The wavelengths of his mind were prone to becoming erratic. He had to take psycho-inventory as well as medication to prevent irrational and erratic behavior, but he had been out of medication for a while now.

Jesus was in the other room, several days into his fast. He sat awake on his bed peering out through the window. The sight of Rivne beyond the window of his room sparked contemplation of humanity. He was not seeing love and care throughout this world for the fellow man through Him, as the Father had planned. Greed may have been the cause, and the world was blind to it. Greed appeared to be a simple co-effect of competition. But, when does one realize he already has enough, and winning isn't everything? When does one realize that this world is not the end, and you cannot take all your worldly possessions with you? The 'Haves' might enjoy the world more than the 'Have Nots,' but to put love of this world and its things first is to put those desires before holiness and the eternal good. That's what sparks greed. It's more than an off-shoot of competition. Greed is blindness to eternal life. Lust for power is blindness to righteousness. Spiritual eternity and the grace and presence of God have the power to deliver joy and pleasure beyond this world, but too few had the faith in this truth. Too many followed the teachings of prophets, professors, and philosophers who spoke to the wants and needs of satisfaction in the here and now. Perpetuating the good of the world and salvation of the spirit were of little concern anymore. The Arabian Bandits didn't care about virtue and goodness. They were just as power-driven and money-hungry as the rest of the world. They violently struggled for sovereignty, seeking punishment and revenge along the way. They were doing their best to punish Rafa and Nick, but the paddlers' spirit was too strong.

Rafa started singing the cartoon song.

"Aaa badabadabadaba," he mocked Haziz as Haziz ranted about the punishment he would bring to the world for his and his people's misfortunes.

"We shall go to Turkey! And pound Turks!"

"Oh, go pound sand," Nick mocked the ring leader.

"It is written!"

"Eh, fuck you,"

Nick never was much of one for scripture.

"Got anymore smoke, dude?" Nick asked Rafa.

"Hey! I am speaking! You will listen!"

"Look, we said we would take you to Jesus. Chill out, ya duffelbag."

"Aghhh gabagabagaba!"

Chapter 20: Reflection

Jesus and his disciples woke up the next day, and took a train from Rivne, Ukraine to the Maramures Mountains at the Ukraine-Romania border. They would not ascend the beautiful mountains, but their majestic power radiated down on the men like a nuclear reactor. They were a symbol, a testament to the power of God. They symbolized the strength in His creation. The Father was the great blacksmith of the landscape, forging features rugged and beautiful, imparting his consciousness unto the creation at hand. Nature seemed to be a reflection of man. Strength and beauty could be seen in both humanity and the natural environment through the apparent imperfections, in the majestic spirituality, and in the ether and ethos that flowed between bodies. Inspiration was felt through the vision of what God had created, and what man could reflect upon. Jesus and his disciples saw this power within themselves. The power of the mountains, the power of God. The Great Creator embodied the world with love and strength from a unified "One," an epicenter. There was a common beginning of it all, and all of it shared character and spirit. As spirit shined down with its energy and consciousness, it became specialized, but retained an amount of its primal source, just enough that a common thread was shared between man and his environment. The divine spirit of God felt obvious as the grandeur of the mountains reflected upon the men. It was as if it had always been there just as a beacon of wisdom, grace, and fertility. Beathan, Kyle, Michael Joseph, Eric, and Todd, none of them were perfect, but each had a spiritual strength that proved valuable. Steadfast strength, innocent perception, love, beautiful stimulation, and wisdom all shined from the five men back on to the mountain, and the mountain smiled.

"I think my fast is over," Jesus said. It was about 10 days since he'd last eaten, and the spirit of the mountains were enough inspiration to feel human once again.

After a nice meal of lamb, cabbage, and potatoes in Romania, the guys were closing in on the Turkish border. They only stopped to eat and drink. Sleep was forgotten about. They were becoming a little delirious, but they weren't exhausted. They were running on spiritual energy. Some say they were running on fumes, but on the contrary, they had fuel. They simply chose to skip the resting cycle. There are two deprivations to human nature that shock the natural psychology of a person. One is lack of food. The other is lack of sleep. When a person is deprived of either one, a new perspective of reality is born within. Jesus had just come off of a long fast, and now he and the boys were neglecting to sleep. Todd needed it the most. Erratic brain waves were causing him to slip into obvious psychosis. He began talking, ranting, and never stopped.

It went on for several minutes before Eric lost his cool.

"Would you Shut Up!" he screamed at his friend.

Todd's head turned so red it looked as if it were going to explode.

Beathan was doing something with his breathing and heart rate as he walked, as if trying to harmonize with something or transform his outer being… shape shifting… skin walking. Michael Joseph and Kyle were just quiet with eyes glued to the horizon, and somber smiles on their faces. They were trudging along, just happy to be, feeling the presence of the Lord. Todd kept yammering, sometimes so quietly that he could barely be heard. His voice was a non-stop monotone that couldn't be understood in any language. Eric was so defeated that he looked like he just got punched in the face. Beathan never stopped trotting and shimmying. The crew went on like this for about 8 hours, through dusk and into the darkness of night. When they arrived at the Turkish border, there were guards standing with rifles.

"What the hell is going on out there!" Patrick Carney exclaimed to the rest of his band as they were waking up in their Istanbul hotel.

Jerry Garcia walked over to the window and saw the city burning.

"Riots. It looks like."

"Nah man, it's worse than that. *This is Jihad,*" Bootsy Collins coolly explained.

"What is it with religion and war? I thought God was supposed to be love, not hate and destruction."

"Maybe they ain't *got* God. *They sure enough ain't getting any of The Odyssey.*"

Jerry phoned the tour manager and told him to cancel the show.

Heathens came out of the Arabian desert, delirious from fasting. They raised upheaval to Turkey and the Turkish culture. Allowing The Odyssey to play in their country was sacrilege to middle eastern customs. It was as inconceivable as whitewater kayaking, anything free spirited. It seemed to be a rebellion to the institutions that that region of the world grounded their communities and society. The thought of dancing to western music, and the passions that might derive, enraged those who held faith in the old-world customs. Striking fear and terror into the innocent was the only solution. They accomplished their goal, and chased peace, love, and understanding away from their corner of the world. When word got out that The Odyssey was canceling their last show before Glastonbury, Beathan and Todd took it pretty hard. Their minds were set on something mystical and supernatural as if there was a void that another transcendental show would fill.

"Let's go back to the last town in Romania, and get a place to sleep and drink a few beers," Michael Joseph thoughtfully interjected.

"Sounds like a plan man!" Kyle replied.

Jesus knew he could do nothing to quell the uprising. Christians weren't really welcomed in Turkey. It was a predominantly Islamic state. Now, with western culture set to transcend, Arabian Bandits were coming out of the desert to terrorize the whole country. The desert heathens could not empathize with Christ's mission. Moments of peace and harmony were afoot, now a tribal war was disrupting an event that could change the whole world for the better. The Arabian Bandits spent too much time in a place too dry with too many wives. Then they decided to give up eating and went sun gazing without much truth in their direction. Their integrity was based on fallacy, and they ran headlong like the wind with it. Now, all there was were violence and ruin. The clash was misguided. There would be no peace. The Prince of Peace was the enemy. The boiling self-righteousness of the Arabian Bandits was scalding the delicate skin of peace, love, and understanding. Harmony was not an option. Love for thy neighbor did not exist. The life was not the one Jesus taught. And now pain and death were all that there was.

The mayhem in Turkey had Jesus's five disciples a little distracted, but the Lord kept keen focus on his mission. He had no preconceived notions about how he would be received in Turkey. It turned out that he would not be received at all. But, Haziz and his clan never slowed the chase after the Lord. They were upset about something. Maybe the Arabian Bandits were disgusted with all the failed promises their religion delivered. The principles of their belief were righteous: Profession of Faith, Prayer, Charity, Fasting, and Pilgrimage. Execution and discipline within those principles was where that culture seemed to fail, at least it was failing within the bandits that flooded Istanbul. The principle of charity was lost in the vision for a better world. It was professed, but too much power was handed to fate. Fate without guidance and insight follows the lines of entropy and chaos. There is too much faith that right will be made right without sacrifices of time, talent, and energy. But, without making peace and adhering to discipline, the greedy-strong will feed on the weak, and disrupt the balance of love and harmony. This disruption leaves the disenfranchised angry and hate-filled, and now some of those angered were out to seek revenge on a grudge that was centuries old.

At one time, Christians were the greedy-strong feeding on the weak Arabians. Centuries of contempt led Haziz and his crew to mar Christian culture. Jesus figured someone would be in the way of his call out to the hippies who came from generations of Christian blood. The hip-call was the same as His call: peace, love, and understanding. Opening your eyes to what is happening. The creed of empathy did not make hip culture any more palatable for Haziz and his Arabian Bandits. Haziz connected Jesus to the root of it all. And, Jesus figured the ones who would oppose him would be a people who felt that they were never among the chosen-ones, and looked for righteousness elsewhere. But Christ was on a mission, and a rather groovy one at the moment. A little high, a little harmony, and immeasurable power in the Holy Spirit.

By the time they made it back to Romania, Beathan was looking a bit out of sorts. It had been a few weeks since Todd had taken any medication, and the two of them were slipping off into hallucinations and pagan delusions. They were feeling the weight of the road. There was little substance to fuel their fight towards the goal. Thoughts of where they had been and what they had seen were ruminating in their minds. Despite the righteousness of their directive, Todd was knee-deep in mania, and Beathan was having trouble maintaining the connection between the Spirit and Christ. Beathan was a bit tripped out. His lack of worship left his faith and understanding weak and impressionable to the forces along the trek. Dangerous. Yet, they tried to hold onto faith, whatever that meant to them. It was something different for everyone. Todd's faith was the deepest, but he was manic and periodically ranting with psychotic heresy without his meds. He was citing scripture and beginning to lose sight of the reality that was before him. He focused on the written prophecy, talking about details of the second-coming and forgetting the mission at hand: peace, love, and understanding, and a profession of faith. He was moved, and becoming hard to communicate with. Michael Joseph didn't lack faith, but he never asked to be part of this journey. It was a bit much, and he didn't know what to do, or how to do it. The most he could do was follow Christ, and just take it one day at time. Kyle was a believer, but the convictions in what he was chasing were obscure to him. He couldn't visualize what he was trying to accomplish, but it was naturally occurring within him all along. He just needed a little guidance. He needed to leave some of his psychedelic and perverse passions behind. The presence of Christ was moving strongly within him. He felt incredible inner peace and strength. It was more transcendental even than that night in Helsinki, seeing The Odyssey. Eric had faith, but his passion for Christ hadn't matured. He didn't thirst for the spirit. He wanted sensual gratification, not spiritual salvation, nor utilitarian pleasures. Beathan knew Christ as little more than a man he was traveling with. All of Beathan's spirituality was just what could be gathered from the earth before him.

    Faith was different for everyone, but it was based in the belief that Christ was the Son of God, infallible and all knowing. Christ was a man, a symbol of the embodiment of God in the form of his most-loved creation, humans. He suffered and accomplished everything a man could be asked of in life. He fasted. He worked miracles, he taught, and he was martyred for the blessing of forgiveness and life everlasting. The most important part of faith was to follow Christ's teachings, and never doubt the power of the Father, Son, and Holy Spirit. With faith in Christ, there is more hope and more power to overcome the challenges of life. Faith was more than just being a decent human being. It is often said that a tree is identified by its fruit, and if the fruit of a man is righteous and holy, then so is he. Eric, Todd, Michael Joseph, Kyle and Beathan were on their faith journey. For some of them it was new. For some of them it changed their character, but it was hard to focus upon. When Christ was with them, focusing was easy. When they chased their own wants and desires, some of the men lost sight of Jesus.

Chapter 21: Shave Your Head

The men were looking for a way out of Romania. They managed to find a line from Craiova, Romania to Budapest, Hungary. They were a long ways from Glastonbury, England. The rails were rickety. Lights flickered as the train rolled down the tracks. Click-clack, click-clack. Torn seats and tarnished tables filled the cars. As the train crossed over the Carpathian Mountains in the wee hours of morning, the walls rattled, and the lights hardly stayed lit. Spirit was flowing furiously through the clan. They quaked with energy. They wanted to reach out in evangelism. Todd began exclaiming things and exalting the Lord in tongues. Passengers watched with wide eyes, and the conductor threatened to throw them off the train if Todd didn't control himself. He grew angry.

"Todd, remember the book of James. 'Be quick to listen, slow to speak, and slow to anger,'" Jesus spoke to him. "The world needs love, not terror. These people do not need a radical. They are good," he went on.

Todd began to contemplate what defines theology, wisdom, and sanity. There had to be continuity between the three. Surely, his unreasonable behavior wasn't to blame on the faith in a higher power. He was being brutally honest with an amplitude and fervor that was hard to embrace. What made a man wise? Was it insight to truth? Was it the ability to adapt and overcome? Those ideas may have been part of being wise, but for Todd the key to walking through life with wisdom laid in the ability to remain humble. The masses didn't want to hear heralding truth. And the people who did often fought over what the truth was. Kyle, on the other hand, was wise to the truth, but remained quiet about the things he believed. He was no theologian, but knew that God and Jesus were good. Every day, he believed in them more and more, until that night on the train when he accepted Christ as the keeper of his soul. Looking at Todd and Beathan, Kyle could see that, he too, was a sinner and there was no salvation except through Christ. He prayed.

"Lord Jesus, I want the gift of eternal life. I am a sinner, and have been trusting myself. Right now, I renounce my confidence in myself and put my trust in Thee. I accept you as my personal Saviour. I believe you died for my sins, and I want you to come into my life, and save me. I want you to be the Lord and Master of my life. Help me turn from my way and follow you. I am not worthy, but I thank you, Lord, for saving me. Amen."

Kyle was transcending, and could see how broken the world was. He could see the ideology of a soulless world. It was one that only attributed God to morality and ethics. The world saw no use in being passionate about having a personal relationship with Jesus. They just saw no use to being social or vocal about the idea, praising him, or calling on him for strength or comfort. Faith in Christ was a bit more subjective to time, place, and experience. Kyle began to recollect the journey. He recalled the warmth and comfort in places that held Christ close to their hearts. Places like Poland and Lithuania fixed their eyes unto the ways of the Lord, in good times and bad. Through it all, the atmosphere of sustainable-love established itself, and flourished. In environments where faith in Christ is popular, folks are more likely to proclaim their faith. When it is unpopular, the faithful are viewed as psychotic as Todd, off his meds, ranting and exclaiming. The sympathy Kyle felt for Todd was painful as he saw Todd's, as well as Beathan's, habits spiral in a radical and irrational direction. Beathan approached the Lord.

"I think I need to shave my head,"

Beathan's long black braids looked angry, like a heathen, a druid, a witch who couldn't have the spirit of Christ within him. Beathan was barely talking the talk, but wanted to walk to walk. When he looked in the mirror, he wanted to be able to see someone righteous from head to toe. Ever since their trek through the Baltic state, Beathan had been growing stronger in his faith, but it wasn't a linear progression. While God was at work, so was the Devil, trying to snuff out the light of direction and righteousness. The Devil knew the heathen ways Beathan identified with for years, and attempted to enslave him to wickedness. A good haircut would be a step towards looking the part he wished to live. They couldn't do it on the train, though.

Chapter 22: Walking the Walk

They arrived in Austria in daylight. It was a weekday. They were in Rennerdorf, a small town east of Vienna. There were no concerts, no demands for beer. They were on a mission. They split into two groups. Kyle, Beathan, and Michael Joseph were looking for a barber shop so Beathan could get that wild mat of braids chopped off, and Todd, Eric, and Jesus were trying to find some meds for Todd.

"One bad haircut can ruin a man's life," Kyle joked.

"Or it can save his soul for all eternity," Beathan jested.

"Well… Haircut? Good. Faith? Better." Christ philosophized in brevity before the crew separated. There were not a lot of shaved heads in Austria. Most of the men wore their hair neatly trimmed. Only gang bangers sported the chrome-dome. It took some work getting through the dread-locks that matted his mane. Once the hair was cut away and trimmed down to the scalp, Beathan's head needed a thorough washing. The skin was pimply and flakey. The barber lathered him up good and scrubbed away, repeating the practice time after time. Finally, they cured the surface up to something that could be finished with a razor. Beathan left the barber shop with stubble on his head.

"I thought you were going for the reverse hippy? You know, long beard, shaven head."

"I want to finish the trim myself," Beathan said to Kyle with a look of serenity on his face, as though it was something he had been looking forward to.

Beathan, Kyle, and Michael Joseph went off to find Jesus, Eric and Todd who were looking for a psychiatrist who could provide Todd with some antipsychotic medication.

"This shouldn't be a complicated process. He's not asking for painkillers or anxiety medication. He has schizoaffective disorder. He needs an anti-psychotic prescription filled," Eric and Jesus went on trying to prove the truth to Dr. Freud.

"This is unusual for a traveler to be in such demand of something such as this, but I can help. It does not mean I *will help*, but I can. Mister Todd will just have to take a crude examination."

Dr. Freud asked Jesus and Eric to leave the office and began asking Todd questions. They focused on the symptoms.

"Do you hear voices. Do you see shadow figures?"

The doctor started with the hallucinogenic symptoms such as hearing voices and seeing shadow figures, then worked through unwarranted fear and hopelessness, wrapping things up with personal history that might hint towards mania and delusional thinking. Todd was delusional without a doubt. His perception of reality was far from common. Thoughts of supernatural forces constantly filled his mind and engulfed his behavior. He was seeing and hearing things no one else could. It was challenging trying to relate or communicate with him by the time they made it to Rennerdorf. And the manic rants. Todd was not himself. The doctor made his observations and came to a decision.

"Here is a prescription for 30-day supply of olanzapine. Take one 15 milligram tablet every day at bedtime."

"Thanks doc, he needed it!"

Jesus and Eric thanked the doctor, and when they walked out of the psychiatrist's clinic, Michael Joseph, Kyle and Beathan were waiting for the other three.

"Yi! That's different!" Eric exclaimed at Beathan's appearance.

"Feels refreshing to get a little air to that bit of skin." Beathan replied with a grin. "I still need to take a razor to what's left."

They were walking about looking for a drugstore. Beathan needed a shaving kit, and Todd needed to fill his prescription. Eventually they found the drugstore and got what they needed, then went on their way to find a place to spend the night. Funds were running low at this point. They began taking closer notice to how much money they were going through, and how much they had left. Hostels in Vienna cost twice as much as the ones in Rennerdorf. With a room acquired, Beathan lathered his head and started shaving away the stubble. Todd washed down a 15mg pill of olanzapine with a full glass of water. Jesus approached him.

"Meditate with me. These kinds of medicines usually take a while to show effect. Maybe we can accelerate the process."

Jesus and Todd meditated. They had the room to themselves. Todd could feel his stomach growl, and liver sequester and cycle fluids. The pill was entering the bloodstream. He could feel his heart beating, and blood circulated through his body. The medicine found its way to the regions of the brain that needed it most. Todd remained as calm as he could, and let the molecules of olanzapine deposit into the cells and tissue. After 35 minutes of stillness and slow rhythmic breathing, they opened their eyes, and got to their feet. Todd's eyes looked heavy. He was drained. One look at him, and you could tell something within had been overworked and needed rest and nourishment.

"I think I'm going to lie down and sleep for a while."

"Good..." Jesus replied with a smile.

Todd slipped off into a deep sleep. As the night went on, the rest of the clan made their way to bed, but no one obtained the rest that Todd did. His brain waves mellowed and harmonized. Hormones balanced, and his heart beat slow and soft. The night went on busy and chaotic outside the walls of the hostel, but within the hostel was a place of rest. Beathan laid his head on the pillow, running his hand across the polished skin. He smiled for he had the Lord in his heart. Eric and Michael Joseph slept silently in dreamland. Kyle laid in bed awake for much of the night. He reflected on the life he was living. The trip had begun to feel long, and the chaos of the adventure was becoming apparent, but he felt at peace. He felt like he was exactly where he needed to be in life. He felt purpose, and a connection to something bigger than himself. Like many others who followed The Odyssey, he often thought there had to be a better way to live. Maybe that better way was through God. Maybe it was something that involved less lust and consumption. Everyone tried to escape the pains of living, but Kyle was beginning to realize that those pains were not unavoidable after seeing the riots in Turkey, and the psychosis within Todd, and the delusional, mystical egotism Beathan was trying to distance himself from. Kyle was fulfilling his duty to God, and the intangible rewards made him feel whole and hope-filled. The good heads he associated with were one their way to making good with their souls. Jesus never turned his back on these people, even those who had forgotten who he is, was, and will always be.

Jesus and his disciples rose at daybreak the next day, all except Todd. He was still sleeping around 7AM when the clan wanted to get back on the road.

"Come on. Rise and shine," Kyle coaxed Todd out of bed.

He was a little groggy but appeared sober. Sleepy was better than a little psychotic. With a little moving and a cup of coffee, Todd regained form.

"It felt so good to *sleep*," Todd expressed over his morning java. Everyone looked surprised, as if overnight he had taken some great transformation. There was moderation in his voice and in his face. He was back to the man he loved being.

"Whoa! I forgot about that!" Todd sounded as he glanced at Beathan's shaven head. "It's like the reverse hippy!"

Kyle just laughed. They walked the morning streets of Rennerdorf with coffee in hand back to the train station. There was urgency, but with a sense of tranquility. There was a calmness. The chaotic blur of red-eyed transit was left in the past. Harmony was restored within the wildest players of the team as they worked on closing ground on England. The five disciples weren't quite sure what they were going to face. Beathan was the only one who had been to the festival before, but that was in an erratically different form of mind, a mind tripped out into the far reaches of obscurity and psychedelia. Jesus was the only one who knew the troubles afoot. He had been watching our world from Heaven since the beginning of time, and took note to the path we humans walked. Once they got to the train station and boarded, they would see nothing but railways until Coquelles, Pas-de-Calais in France, the southern terminal of the Chunnel.

Chapter 23: Chunnel Power

It took 37 hours and over a thousand kilometers to reach Coquelles, Pas-de-Calais from Rennerdorf. The guys were stiff, tired, and groggy, but there was giddiness of anticipation within them. Part of that was from the Chunnel ahead. Some was from the prospect of evangelizing the Glastonbury Music Festival. The Chunnel is 50 kilometers of rail tunneled under the English Channel. The commute can cause anxiety, but Jesus and his five disciples were not nervous. The mission ahead occupied their thoughts instead. They got tickets and boarded the train, and things got rolling. In 20 minutes, they would be in England, but something bad started happening. They could feel the train steam ahead, and it kept gaining speed. And kept gaining speed. The wheels whistled, and the walls rattled. Things felt out of control, and fear was setting into the passengers.

Jesus said to his five,

"Grab hands."

The six men clasped each-others hands. The lights dimmed and the rails rocked. Christ began speaking in Hebrew, but all of his disciples knew what he was saying. It wasn't a prayer of exhilarating excitement. Instead it was a message of comfort, and power, and peace. The passengers on the Chunnel line were getting nervous, and excited over the character of the train under the English Channel. Worry and panic rushed over most of them, then Eric got a strange look in his eye as the middle-aged businessman next to him was sweating bullets, on the verge of hyperventilating.

"Take my hand," Eric said. "Lord, fill us with serenity, and courage." Eric's prayer was short, but he kept the man's hand in his own, and a calmness came over the man. All who ask for the Lord's strength will receive it. Eric filled his neighbor with power over fear, and tranquility spread as the rest of the crew ministered, and worked miracles of tranquility over all of the passengers, as the train appeared to be on the road to nowhere, broke-down in a tunnel under the English Channel. Instead, the train smoked its way onto the shores of England. As the passengers exited, the conductor was amazed at how calm and stable they all appeared after such a scary situation.

"Jesus! What happened?" Kyle exclaimed.

"When we held hands and I prayed, I filled you with the Holy Spirit, giving you the power to spread peace and tranquility. You will need that." Jesus replied.

The guys were still a fairly long way from Glastonbury. The festival was to start the next day, but The Odyssey wouldn't take the stage for another three days.

"How far is Glastonbury from here?" Kyle asked.

"About 325 kilometers," Beathan answered.

"What's that in miles?"

"About 200 miles."

"Let's take a bus."

Chapter 24: Folkestone to Glastonbury

It was late in the day when Jesus and his five disciples walked into the Folkestone bus station. There were hippies from all over Europe and the U.S. making the same trek as them. Backpacks, lived-in clothes, and shaggy hair. Some flying solo, couples, and some in small groups trying to make the last 195 miles to the Glastonbury Music Festival.

"We need six tickets to Canterbury," Beathan asked the woman at the ticket window.

"Seats for tomorrow are all sold out. They earliest you can ride is Friday."

"Okay."

"That will be 45 pounds."

Beathan gave the clerk the money, and she handed him 6 tickets to Canterbury.

"Canterbury?" Todd asked.

"From here, the bus lines connect to Canterbury, then Bristol, then Glastonbury."

"How long does it take?"

"About 9 hours."

"Thank God it doesn't get dark until 10:30."

"Well, what do we do until Friday morning?"

"I'd like to have a roof over my head for these two nights," Kyle expressed to the clan. Tea and salad were all that was consumed

Thursday. The nights in the hostel passed quietly. No beer was drank. The six men shared three rooms, and few words were spoken as each contemplated the future. All the traveling brought them ever so close to their final destination. They could only speculate what they would find. Beathan was beginning to see the works that would be done. He knew the craziness that sometimes consumed the music festival. He knew the bewilderment one could find, and the peace that those bewildered souls sought amidst the depths of despair. The main attraction was the music, but psychedelic drugs were not an innocent accompaniment to the society that was created within the campground. Beathan stayed up at night and reflected about who he was, who he has become, and who he will be. Righteousness had a new meaning for him. It was something less adrenaline filled. Excitement and bewilderment were not what he desired. The peace that now lived within him was cherished, and life seemed impossible without it.

Eventually Friday came, and the boys rolled out of bed around 5 AM. Todd was still a bit groggy, but the sun was high, and the road called. They made their way to the bus station, and boarded. The ride was quiet. Most of the passengers aboard were following the same route as Jesus and his disciples. In a few hours they would transfer lines at Canterbury, then a few hours later they would make their final transfer in Bristol.

The busses to Canterbury then Bristol were crowded and hot. Not a lot of conversation. The discomfort from the English summer made an environment that stifled the mind from socializing with strangers. Instead the focus was on whatever breeze could be felt from the cracked bus windows.

They made it to Bristol and boarded the final bus. The crew could feel themselves closing in on the music festival. The passengers were almost entirely hippies headed to Glastonbury. One in particular was seated across the aisle from Michael Joseph and Todd. His name was Nathan.

"Man, I've been seeing The Odyssey since back in the 90's, caught almost every tour! There's been some good acid going around this summer. I was trippin' at the show in Helsinki, and saw a guy turn into a thunder cloud."

Todd thought to himself, "If Nathan only knew."

"I bet there's gonna be some good stuff in Glastonbury. A righteous show with a headful of acid… nothin' better! Good vibes all the way!"

Todd couldn't contain himself anymore.

"Have you ever seen a show without any drugs?"

"Ha! That's sacrilege!"

"No, man. Have you ever gone to see natural vibes? My crew and I have been to a few shows this summer. No drugs. I don't know if I'd call the concerts righteous, but we were rolling on some pretty heady vibes!"

"Oh, man! You don't know what you're missing out on. It's like cosmic energy."

"Like the Holy Spirit?"

"What are you talking about?"

Todd pointed to Jesus seated two rows ahead of him and Nathan.

"Who's that guy?"

"The Prince of Peace."

"That's a pretty boastful handle."

Todd let Nathan revel in his own wonder, for Todd knew the power of the Holy Spirit. Nathan's ignorance was truly bliss. The denial of spirit and the embrace of cosmic energy with no guiding consciousness was the hip call to a higher power that held no power at all. What could it mean, cosmic energy? Was it the force that flowed throughout universe unaware of itself, but acknowledging those it laid itself upon? What force could sympathize without a sense of self-awareness? Was it pride or ego that halted the acceptance of a conscious spirit, energy and consciousness coupled into a single, holistic force, sympathizing, spreading peace and joy, strength and love, throughout the world? Todd got a little taste of the people and community he was about to enter. It was an unknown, unexperienced realm to him at that point, but Todd had to grasp an understanding of their ideology. How could such a serene and ethereal environment choose to ignore the present, and not accept the blessed power of God?

The bus out of Bristol was closing in on Glastonbury late Friday.

"Guys, we're almost there," Beathan explained with giddiness. The small stone houses and lush green field of the English countryside passed by the bus windows for a few more miles. The bus pulled into the town of Glastonbury on a hot dry evening. Everyone got off, and Jesus and his disciples began following the crowd through the streets. The buildings were small, and everything looked like it was built in the middle-ages.

"I'm starving. We gotta eat," Eric said to the gang with more stamina than usual, despite being drained of fuel.

"There's a few bakeries that sell pasties."

"Pasties?"

"Yeah. They're like a hot sandwich wrapped in a flaky crust. Perfect to eat on the go."

The crowd shrugged at Beathan's words, but they sounded like a good idea. They walked to Beathan's favorite place for the dish. There was a glow within the place somewhere between trippy and supernatural. Shadows had an electric luminescence, and the light that filled the room was soft, almost a wee bit dim. There was a balance of energy. The deli counter was the only thing that was really bright. The only deli worker behind the counter was a short girl with red hair. Her age could not be identified. She had a beauty that was possible at any age. Her skin tone said 20, but the lines on her face and silver in her strawberry-blond hair suggested the possibility of over 60. Her voice was perky in tone, but slow in meter. The disciples couldn't decide if she was the image of excitement or tranquility. They all ordered sausage, egg, and cheese pasties, and walked out in a confusion of delight. There was an appeal about the girl that spoke to the soul of each man. Was it an attraction that was simply aesthetic, or was the feeling something intrinsic and transcendental, innocence and beauty that spoke to the soul?

Jesus and his disciples munched as they followed signs out of town and to the festival. A mile of cars lined the trail back to the campground. Little coupes with gear packed on the rooves and Volkswagen Microbusses could be seen all along the way. Still, many were coming in on foot. Shaggy heads and backpacks trotted to the gate where Jesus and the disciples would enter the festival.

"What about tickets?" Todd asked everyone.

"These should work," Jesus said as he held out six passes into the Glastonbury Music Festival.

"What *can't* you do?" Kyle jostled.

"Hm."

They walked through the entrance, and headed to the campground. Music could be heard all the way across the property. It sounded like Franz Ferdinand was on stage at the moment. They walked past tents, campers, and canopies with British alternative rock rolling through the hot summer air. The temperature wasn't sweltering, but Kyle and Beathan had sweat beading on their foreheads as they trotted along with packs on their backs. Eyes squinted in the sun as they took in their surroundings. They were finally there. The Glastonbury Music Festival, where sensual pleasure came in numerous commodities. It wasn't vice-land or sin-city, but it was far from righteous, despite what many there might have thought. Despite the indulgences, Jesus saw something in the people who formed this community, something that revolved around the joy of being alive, and the love and care for others. It was a community that was not selfish. It was not ignorant. It was just misguided, and lacked sound direction. Many good notions existed in the minds of these people, but a foundation of theological faith was something that was scarce among them. This was the salt of the Earth, the congregation the Lord longed for. These were not people trying to control God through begrudging obedience. These were people living in the moment, but the moment was, at times, perverse, vile, and even painful. Todd just shook his head as he walked through the community of alternative lifestyles. "What could be gained? What did He want *these* people for?" Todd thought. The answer was dynamic. It was not a simple "yes" or "no". It was something that laid within human passions. Like everyone else, these hippies longed for comfort. Some of which could be found in a beer, a joint, or a cup of coffee. The rest of that comfort came from having a relationship with God. That's what Christ was there for, to show there was comfort and strength in the Lord when you called upon his presence. He was the way, the truth, and the life; a face and soul to build a relationship with. The music was fun, even exciting at times, but was it excitement, or tranquility, which joy thrived within? Possibly a combination of the two. The Prince of Peace was waist deep in a heady rock festival. Speaking a life of discipline could not have been done in a harder place. What *could* be relative was a life of passion.

Chapter 25: Chaos in Glastonbury

"Hey, son. whatchya rollin'?" Kyle asked as he passed three people sparking up a joint. It wasn't intentional. It was a shear instinctive reaction when the skunky herb hit his nostrils.

"Darek's got some White Widow, and I saved a little Purple Haze from Amsterdam." Kyle grinned, and glanced over at the Lord who shook his head with a little disappointment.

"You want in on this?" the boy asked.

Kyle took a minute to calculate the lateral preferences.

"Can't right now…" he said with regret.

Kyle caught up with the rest of the disciples and came to Christ.

"What's allowed?"

"Faith and repentance. If you feel guilt, abstain. I'm not here to tell you that you can't enjoy life. Just know I died the death every man deserved to die."

Kyle took the words pretty heavy. That's a tough reality to accept, knowing how flawed, how unacceptable your actions and your desires really are. Kyle went into his head for a while. Jesus and the disciples kept walking along.

"What are we looking for?" Eric asked.

"It's in front of us. We just need a thorough understanding," Jesus replied.

Everyone had a glaze of satisfaction. "You see these people? They are no different than any man, every man. Just the faces of the human races. But they got soul. I just wonder if they perceive me as a myth…"

"You're no myth!" a few of the disciples responded in unison. The congregated-response brought Kyle back from his thoughts. He laughed a little chuckle, then approached the Lord.

"Hey man, I'm gonna smoke. Maybe not right now, but this place only appears in truth to me with a little bit of pot."

"Kyle, in Proverbs 31 it is professed, 'Give strong drink to him that is ready to perish, and wine to those that be of heavy hearts…'"

"So..?"

"Wine, Kyle. Wine."

Kyle still couldn't make any sense of it. None of the men could, except Todd, but Todd wasn't paying attention.

"Did you get any of that?" Kyle asked Todd as they continued to meander through the village of encampments.

"Any of what? I wasn't paying attention."

Kyle had enough. He unshouldered his bag as they walked, and with keen dexterity, he rolled a little joint as they moved on foot. He fired up the pinner, and took a few long drags, unable to really indulge in the activity.

"I guess you figured it out…" Jesus said to Kyle with a soft look in his eyes.

Kyle toked away at that little cigarette filled with sticky green bud, and energy could be sensed flowing. It came from the people, and reflected the music, the environment, and every element of conscious stimulation that existed within the festival. The spirit could be sensed. It wasn't dumb-ether. It was more than cosmic energy. It was divine energy-and-consciousness. Kyle walked along the dusty roads with a heightened sense of perception. Faces appeared a bit wily, but ever so welcoming. There was a vague sense of misdirection heard in the banter of the festivalgoers. Obscurity and deviation from truth might have been the activation energy that sent hip culture spiraling away from righteous spirituality in a wholistic sense of the term. But, they had everything else, fervor and thirst for life, love and compassion, morals. Well, kind of. When mind expansion comes at the cost of the health or well-being of others, then it becomes immoral. Otherwise, one is not to become a waste of life. Suppose that is the philosophical truth. Kyle passed the joint to Michael Joseph who took one really heavy drag off the pinner, and began grooving. The Arctic Monkeys were taking the stage, and the whole campground was in transition. Everyone was getting ready for the Friday night headliner. 135,000 campers flocked to the green fields of the English countryside. Michael Joseph and Kyle took lead and began following hippies to the stage. The mob funneled down as they progressed toward stage front, and Eric began to get a good idea of what Christ was after, 135,000 kind hearts.

"There's so many people!" Eric gasped.

"This is a good start…" Jesus replied.

"Are they all lost?" Todd asked.

"Hm." Jesus replied.

The Arctic Monkeys opened with the song 'Arabella.' The music harmonized in cool mystique. The eerie vibes resonated with bold passion. The set would go on for 90 minutes. Everyone was high, but soon the music would be over, and the festivalgoers would be left with nothing more than their own souls for warmth and happiness. At the end of the night, some would be at peace. Some would not. Some knew Christ. Some did not.

Jesus and his disciples left the stage front as the music ended.

"Got a tent in that bag?" Jesus asked Beathan.

"What do you think?" Beathan replied with a smile.

They worked their way back through camp, and set up two three-man tents. The six of them crawled in and laid down. Shrieks of excitement and crazed conversations could be heard through the night. Todd, who was usually out cold within an hour of taking his medication, laid awake in the tent, and listened to the community through the night. Sometimes he slipped deep into thought. "Some of these people know Christ." Glastonbury was a far cry from southern California. These were not the streets of L.A. Likewise, this was not Eastern Europe. There was an array of spirituality that existed within this mob of people. Todd really couldn't wrap his mind around it all. He existed on one extreme or the other, and he thought that's how the whole world existed, but that was not how the whole world existed. Todd could hear Beathan talking in his sleep.

"Who chased the hobbit out of the butcher shop?"

Todd chuckled a little bit. What could it mean? But he thought more about the spectrum of faith. It was before him the whole time, spanning from Beathan to Michael Joseph and himself. Atheists, lukewarm Christians, and the spiritually devout. Some souls burned with a fiery passion, blazing with faith and smoldering with repentance. Todd felt a little less righteous in the moment. It was not he that saved lost souls. It was simply his call to lost souls to start a relationship with God that saved. That humble circumstance did not make him less of a man. It only made him question and contemplate his own identity.

He had to get up to answer nature's call. As he walked through the night, alone, to the porta-john, he saw a young man with a fear-crazed look in his eye. The young man was trotting fast and pulling at his hair. Todd responded true to his nature.

"Hey man, what's wrong?"

"I took some acid, and couldn't handle the tent anymore, so I went for a walk, now I can't find my way back, and everyone is talking about me, and I think a couple people were planning on robbing me. I don't feel safe. How long does this stuff last?"

"What's your name, man?"

"Justin."

"You thirsty, Justin? Let's walk to market and get a bottle of water."

"But that's at the other end of camp, and I don't know how to get back, and…"

"Pray with me, Justin."

Justin rubbed his brow a little bit, then took Todd's outstretched hand, and Todd began praying.

"God, we are in a moment of despair, fear, and weakness. Please bring Justin strength, peace, and comfort. Amen"

Spirit flowed from Christ as he laid asleep in his tent, and filled Justin. The acid didn't slow down. Dude was trippin' balls.

"How much acid did you eat?"

"A ten strip. They looked so little, I thought I'd need a few of them."

Todd knew the hardline Justin might have to walk. He could only hope his prayer would deliver Justin.

"So, do you believe the Jesus guy is real?"

Justin seemed to be calming down.

"I live with him every day," Todd replied with a wry grin. Todd could feel the energy coming off of Justin. He had confidence his prayers were being answered, but Justin was the only one who could really tell. The two of them gazed at the stars through the indigo night. It was a rather peaceful moment, despite the circumstances.

"Do you even know where we're at?" Justin asked.

"Glastonbury."

"I meant where at in camp."

"Hm."

They were closing in on the market where they could buy a bottle of water.

"Feeling better?" Todd asked with hesitation, fearful of the truth.

"I am. Crazy! It's like I feel... I feel ..."

"Strength, peace, and comfort?"

"Yeah!"

"If you keep the Lord in your life, he will answer your prayers, especially when you ask for strength... when you ask for his presence."

They got some water, and Todd bought a little bit of hot food. Justin still had some inner tension keeping him from developing any kind of appetite.

"Think you know where to find your tent?"

"Yeah, things are looking a little more familiar," Justin answered with a bit of a chuckle. "I'm camped pretty close to where you found me."

"Cool. Let's head back."

There wasn't a lot of conversation, but Todd felt a sense of satisfaction. His prayers were answered, and the healing wasn't even for himself. He saw the spirit work within one around him. That made it even more satisfying, to serve others.

"I think the stuff is wearing off. I see my tent."

"Cool."

Todd knew that it could just be a wave of the trip declining. Justin would ride a few more waves before dawn, but maybe not. Maybe the Holy Spirit would work a miracle of sobriety. Maybe God would let Justin ride the waves of the trip until everything wore off.

"Well, thanks for everything! Maybe I'll see ya around," Justin farewelled.

"Remember the Lord. Peace be with you."

Justin grinned a little and shook his head as the two parted ways.

It was now around 4:00 AM Saturday morning. Pre-dawn light was fading in, and Todd could hear Beathan yawning. He stood outside for a few minutes to see if anyone would come out of the tent. It didn't take long before Beathan's brawny frame crawled out, rubbing his bald head and scratching his beard.

"Good morning."

"Good morning."

"Do you have the stuff to make coffee, Beathan?"

"As a matter of fact..." the Scotsman said with a smile.

"Yeah?"

"Yeah."

Beathan began digging through his pack for the stove, pot, and coffee. He lit the burner, and filled the coffee pot. The two of them waited for the water to percolate. Watching dawn break in the English countryside was a new experience for Todd. He was a bit in awe with child-like astonishment. Conversely, Beathan was in his element, that time and place we have grown accustomed to, the environment we have been conditioned to feel most in place. This was just one of many British sunrises for Beathan.

"This is a little different than L.A." Todd said, breaking the silence.

Beathan took a long moment before saying anything.

"I'd guess, there, you wake up too fast."

Todd smiled at the remark.

"If you progress slowly, you gain more from each moment. Mornings in the Highlands are where I feel… God, I guess. I'm just not sure how man, society, is connected to it. I couldn't really see where Jesus fit into that."

Todd let Beathan reflect on the idea. He was getting better at listening now that he was back on his medication. As Beathan sat in reflection, Todd reflected a bit himself. In that moment, creation became more than society and all the problems man has built. Spirit was more than emotion. And, peace was real. Before long the coffee was percolating, and Todd and Beathan each poured themselves a cup. They sat, sipping their coffee, together, and watched the campground come to life. The late-night set had only ended three hours earlier, but hippies from all over the Western world were stirring, soaking-in whatever got them awake.

Pot-smoke filled the air as Eric, Kyle, and Michael Joseph crawled out of bed. The Lord was still sleeping, and the hour was approaching 7:00 AM. The early hour of dawn had long passed, and the sun was high in the sky by the time the last of the clan rose to their feet. Clouds moved in, and it looked like rain. "Who chased the hobbit from the butcher shop!" the Lord shouted with gusto, waking himself at the volume of his own voice. His eyes popped open, he did a double take, then laughed a little bit at his own words. Upon his shouting, the clouds cleared, and sun filled the sky. "What kind of man is this that the weather obeys his words?" the disciples thought. A few euro-hippies were within ear-shot and looked at each other, humored with astonishment. Christ crawled out of the tent just before the last cup of coffee was drank.

"Let us pray," Christ started. They all clasped hands, and Jesus spoke. "Heavenly Father, we give thanks for the sun that feeds the crops and fuels the rain that feeds us. May you bless the food, the drink, the smoke, the vibes, and every soul on this Earth. Amen." The disciples were a bit taken by his prayer, but it was better than any other they had ever heard. With the smoke blessed, Kyle fired up a pipe and passed it around. They all hit it except for Eric and Christ.

"I hope that was a good idea," Todd said in hindsight, thinking of his mental disability.

"Just keep breathin', brother," Kyle advised. "You'll be fine. You're free! Glory be!"

The words reminded Todd of the time spent behind bars and in behavioral health institutions. The moment of reflection sent him into a state of gratitude that few men will ever know, to walk through filth and come out clean on the other side.

"Let us walk," Christ said.

They began ambling down the dirt road with the Holy Spirit stirring in them.

"Music doesn't start for another four hours. What do you guys want to do?" Beathan asked.

"Just take it all in. Someone might need us. We might need the flow."

Things started off quietly as they strolled through camp early in the day. Laughter and chatter could be heard as the crew passed encampments, smiling faces, and the occasional cough from a toke off a bowl. Jesus was enjoying the morning with his disciples until a few haughty heads began ridiculing him. They laughed at his robe and were in disbelief of his face, his whole appearance.

"Jesus called. He wants his hair back."

Jesus paused for a moment then looked at the young men, and said,

"Peace be with you," with sincere love and grace. Upon speaking those words, the sun shifted. The light refracted a little bit, and camp began to fill with an ethereal energy. Butterflies danced on the breeze, and trees and grass swayed gently in the soft glow of the day. Peace filled the air as the landscape twinkled with vividness. Festivalgoers were taking notice of Jesus with growing respect and preponderance of the truth as he passed. The rhythm of the day followed them, and pulsated in waves. The soul and spirit of the Glastonbury Music Festival were falling into harmony with Christ and the Holy Spirit. Maybe an hour passed in the splendor of God. The disciples were taking delight in the presence of the Lord. They knew this magical world was the work of their God, and rejoiced. Life was beautiful, but after a while storm clouds began to roll in, and the breeze turned into a cold, stiff wind. The atmosphere evolved into an eerie graveness.

The bitter weather chilled the crowd, then gunshots and the roar of engines were heard off in the distance. They, them. The Arabian

Bandits had made it out of Turkey and across Europe. Now they were storming through the front gates of the Glastonbury Music Festival in jeeps with guns blazing. They managed to subdue Nick and Rafa into tightly sealed water jars, and were on their way to take Jesus captive. Like Christ and his disciples, evil had a mission as well, and both culminated where the salt of the Earth gathered to celebrate life.

"I feel something evil," Todd said to the crew with squinted eyes. A shiver ran down his spine with an impulse of intimidation. He didn't panic. Instead, he was poised for battle. Beathan keened in on Todd's posture, and began scoping the horizon for possible threats.

"Keeping the peace does not mean sitting idly by while tyrants reign in terror." Before Jesus could finish speaking, Beathan was out of sight.

"Where did that Bavarian Druid get to?" Kyle asked, rhetorically.

"Christ, what do we do? Do you think someone is after us?"

"Something tells me my hour has come."

Jesus began walking towards the loud noise of the jeeps. He was not looking for a fight, but was facing the adversity of hatred. Panic and fear could be sensed throughout the place as the five of them walked towards the commotion. Thunder rolled, and the earth trembled under foot with each step Christ took. The world felt hollow. A sense of emptiness was draining the soul of Glastonbury as terrorists moved in upon the festival. Christ stood his ground with determination to fight the good fight. He knew his hands were more powerful than any work of evil, and he was about to prove it once more. Tyranny, evil, and hatred struck a primal nerve with everyone there, even those in the depths of blind hopelessness as last night's drugs were wearing off. One pain overpowered the other as the brain and the spine convulsed with instinct. Christ could feel the distress in full effect. The after-effect of consumption was all Christ was hoping to save these people from, but the evils of society had evolved into something far greater. Now Jesus was about to face that problem, too.

Jesus marched towards the chaos with his disciples following close behind. Some of them felt as though they were marching straight into their death. Some were fearless with the faith of Christ steadfast in their soul. It didn't take long before the five of them held a line before a convoy of Arabian Bandits. Jesus in white robe, long dark hair, and dark beard. Kyle with sandy blond curls. Burly Michael Joseph. Crazy Todd. And meek Eric. And Beathan. Where was Beathan?

"Are you the one they call Jesus Christ!" Haziz shouted at Jesus, and his disciples.

"I am the Son of God," Christ replied coolly in power.

"God has no sons!" Haziz started, garbling in factions, and cocking his assault rifle.

There were a pair of men, wookie-looking types, stoned beyond the impulses of self-preservation witnessing the hostility.

"What are they so mad about?"

"They don't like Jesus, dude."

"Well, it's not like he's here."

"I don't know, man. Did you see the guy in the white robe?"

Haziz was furious, ready to start the assault. About that time, Beathan was sneaking between tents with a blow gun and poison darts. With keen skill, he sent a dart right into Haziz's neck. His eyes rolled back into his head, and Haziz dropped like a sack of potatoes. Thunder cracked violently.

The confusion intensified, and feeling threatened, Ahmed picked up his machine gun, and fired a burst toward Christ without taking aim. Shrieks and cries of fear could be heard all around. The crowd scrambled. A few unfortunate souls were hit with Ahmed's gun fire. Three festivalgoers were wounded. They were bleeding heavily, and one young lady sustained a bullet wound to the chest. Things didn't look good. The injuries caught the attention of those nearby. Jesus was aware, and knew he had to do something. He quickly made his way over to the young lady with the chest wound. Ahmed took a second to train the rifle unto Jesus as he knelt over the bleeding girl. Wooks were enraged, and hippies stood in fear amidst the bloodshed. Tie-dye wearing, dred-lock sporting wooks closed in on the bandits with fire in their eyes, ready to kill. They were armed with whiskey bottles, furious, and ready to strike with retribution. Ahmed was beginning to fear. And, as he was ready to pull the trigger a second time, lightening shot down from the sky and struck Ahmed's jeep. Bright light exploded, and intense heat flashed. The whole convoy of Arabian Bandits were electrocuted as smoke rolled off their charred bodies. The threat had been neutralized, but there were still victims who needed medical attention, one with fatal injuries.

Jesus laid his hands on the young lady's wounds. Brilliant gold light glowed from his hands, and ambient sounds emanated through the airways. Her eyes fluttered a bit. Then the bleeding stopped, and color began to return to her face. She cleared her throat, and stretched her neck again, then smiled. The smile turned to tears as she wrapped her arms around Christ, thankful for the miracle of salvation. She was in shock, experiencing far more than any person should be asked to. Christ shared the embrace for as long as he could, but wanted to cure the wounds of the other two victims.

"Peace be with you," he said as he untangled himself from her arms, and her friends rushed in to comfort her.

About that time, The Odyssey's tour bus was pulling in to the festival. The chaos of terrorism was all about the place, and the band couldn't help but inquire.

"What the hell is goin on! Violence is everywhere!" Brittany Howard questioned with a bit of fury.

"I heard it's some Arabian Bandits causing all the trouble… Maybe it's those same assholes that were blowing up Turkey," Patrick Carney replied.

"Keep the bus running. I'm not sure we're even going to get off," Jerry told the bus driver as they parked. He was debating with himself whether or not the gig was worth the danger.

Jesus was still working on healing the victims wounded by gunfire. One was a 20-year-old man with long straight black hair, thinly built, wearing tight blue jeans, a tight black shirt, and a silver cross around his neck.

"Help the other fella. The bullet passed right through my calf. I'll be alright."

"Bless you."

Jesus walked over to the other man. Tie-dye, big gut, dredlocks. The man would have scoffed at the mention of Christ in any other situation, but now that he was before the man, and needing help, he begged for healing.

"C'mon man! I'm dying here! Do something!"

"Bless you, and bless your enemies, Malchus."

At his spoken words, alone, the man was healed.

"Who's Malchus?" the man's friends asked amongst themselves.

There was much confusion, but the chaos was subsiding. Jesus came back to the victim in blue jeans, and laid his hands on the young man's leg. Soft light emanated from his hands, and a look of relief came to the young man's face. Pain and injury were healed.

"Sir, what is your name?" Jesus asked after laying hands upon him.

"Jason. Thank you, Lord."

Jason stuck around for a few moments just as Beathan was returning from his performance as a vigilante. Beathan was confused at the way Christ treated the wook screaming out at the Lord for healing.

"Why did you treat that man?"

"He needed help."

"Okay. But why would you decree to bless the enemy?"

"If they are not for us Beathan, they are against us. And that multitude is many. Why should I refuse any man if my mission is to save every man, godless hippies and Arabian Bandits, alike. They are no different than the businessman you called soulless at the park in Munich. May they all see the light. May they all have the passion to fulfill God's word."

Jason stuck around to hear what the Lord had say, then quietly moseyed on once the clan had gone silent. Light refracted again, and groovy guitar waves began to fill the air. Christ smiled.

"Hey Kyle, can you twist up a left-handed cigarette?" the Lord inquired.

"Sure thing, boss!"

With keen dexterity, Kyle rolled a beautiful, fat joint. He sparked it up and took a few good tokes off the bone.

"It is a burnt offering, a sacrifice made by fire, of a sweet savor unto the Lord," said Christ as Kyle passed the doober over to him. Christ pinched the joint as if he had done it a thousand times, taking a few nice tokes.

Chapter 26: This Vibe

The Odyssey was still in their tour bus on festival grounds. There wasn't much debate between band mates as to whether or not to play the gig, but there was much contemplation within each member as to the value of the mission of headlining Glastonbury Music Festival at this point. With all the violence and chaos, why risk life and limb just to put on a rock and roll show? Jerry Garcia was nodding off in the back of the bus while Brittany Howard looked out the window. The weather was beautiful on that English summer's afternoon. She opened the door of the bus, and stepped out into the sunshine. Something felt strange, real weird, like a high she never knew existed, but one she always wanted. Something just felt right, keen, vivid, and welcoming. She could taste the calm in the air. It felt like that moment when everything was in its place. There was a frequency about the place that rolled on a harmonizing wavelength, and spoke to every soul, whispering truths of belonging. Brittany Howard's mind was made up. No matter what some Arabian Bandits were doing, she was going to play the show. If none of the band was with her, oh well. She'd solo.

"Guys, catch *this* vibe," she said to the rest of the band as she stepped back inside the bus. They all filed outside. When Patrick Carney hit the lawn, he was cheesin' like a geek.

"Man… It's like I always told you guys…" Jerry started, unable to finish the thought. If he could, he probably would have said something about love, passion, and harmony. Stoic wisdom laid itself upon the minds of all the bandmates. It was something apart from rationale and intellect. It was wisdom that focused on compassion, not pride. Jerry recounted the initial thought.

"… just have faith in Jesus." Jerry finally finished, surprised at his own conclusion. They all giggled a bit, but there was an element of truth intrinsic to the statement, truth that each one instinctively accepted, and generally embraced. They viewed the world around them with the unpolluted perception of a child. But, was it them tripped out, or was the world around them coalescing into something more beautiful, minute by minute?

On the other side of camp, Jesus and his disciples were walking, smiling. Then the wine ran out.

"What do you mean you only brought three fifths?"

"I didn't want to spend too much. I thought that would last us."

Jesus and his disciples overheard a young hip couple arguing.

"This is a music festival! We could go three *gallons* of wine through the weekend!"

Jesus intervened.

"Stop arguing."

"Man…"

"Stop."

The guy quieted down with a grumpy look on his face.

"Do you have any water?"

"Yeah."

"Bring it to me."

The man brought a gallon jug of water, and handed it to Jesus. Jesus gave it a shake and hummed something, and the water changed to a dark red merlot.

"Drink." Jesus held the jug out to the man.

Baffled, the man took a sip.

"Wow! That's good! Are you? Are you?"

"Yes, I'm the Son of God."

"Hallelujah!"

Within earshot, two wooks could be heard having a conversation. Something was in debate.

"Man, I don't care how many shows you've been to. Music is *not counted*. It is *listened to…*"

Jesus laughed at the conversation. All disagreements quelled as the festival gained faith in the truth and power of Christ. His righteousness was endearing, and more and more were beginning to believe that he was more than some tall tale from ancient history.

The passions of the festival goers were evolving in a righteous direction. They were developing harmony with the world around them, both sensual and transcendental, both spiritual and physical. The kingdom of God was upon the Glastonbury Music Festival. All the distance that God put between himself and his people for punishment of original sin had been dissolved upon Christ's return, and his venture into the central nervous system of hip culture. What was once emptiness was now being filled with the grace of God, as the salt of the Earth converged upon righteous vibrations. The mantra of hip culture, peace, love, and understanding, was being paired with faith in God's righteous Son, and the world was pulsating with the energy and consciousness of the Holy Spirit. The landscape was angelic, and the diet of grooves was taken on with a passion for life. The here and now was not pious, but the presence of Christ, and his love for these people was enough to bring righteousness, and harmony on an ethereal level. The sky was a metallic teal with gold light filtering down through the atmosphere. Plants and grasses glowed bright green, and the ground was soft under foot. The fellowship of the festivalgoers became honest, and respectable. The jive misdirection of sassy hippies had been forgotten in a quick transformation of soul as passions evolved into value and validation of the fellow man. Everyone burned with love, zest, and excitement of the Holy Spirit and celebration of the human dimension. Love came to fruition. It was not only claimed, it was proven as everyone sympathized and encouraged each other, celebrating life with appreciation for the Creator. The world that was once harsh and demanding was now giving back to the desires of men and women. Everything seemed in place, perfect. They kept walking along, and came to a man who looked out of place, very out of place. He was dressed like an old English butcher outfitted with a wooden wagon of meat standing next to a stone grill.

"*Who are you?*" Beathan asked with confusion, trying not to be too abrasive.

"Marcus! I have fattened calf!" Marcus held out a plate of thick steak with brilliant marbling. Beathan reluctantly accepted, and dug in with fork and knife. His eyes got big, and a smile grew on his face. He gleefully nodded in approval to both Christ and Marcus. Beathan said not a word, and continued to chow down vehemently.

"Come eat!" Christ yelled, his voice echoing the whole way across the 300-acre campground. A few nearby quickly made their way over to Marcus and his fattened calf. The steaks were thick and juicy. The tongue exploded with flavor, as hippies feasted on the succulent meat. And as more people were served, more and more lined up. Not only was there smoke and drink, but luxurious meals that costed nothing. Everyone was enjoying the food and atmosphere. Hate and famine were forgotten, and it felt as though they would never return. All the burdens of the world had vanished and everyone was at the brilliant feast of mind, body, and spirit. It was the feast of rapture. It was the homecoming of Christ, and the deliverance of mankind back to the Creator. Wine was flowing as people ate, drank, and smoked in the glow of the day as the music played. It was a time of great jubilation. Then, Jesus pulled Beathan aside and whispered something in his ear. Beathan shrugged as Jesus handed him a water jug. He began shaking it and shouted,

"Thou shall not suffer the lack of salt of any of the meat offerings! With all thine offerings, thou shalt offer salt!"

When he was finished Beathan's heart was pounding, and he was a little short of breath. In the jug sloshed a dark amber ale.

"May I?" Beathan asked. Christ nodded and Beathan took a sip.

"Delicious!"

It was an old-ale whose recipe had been long forgotten through the annals of time.

"Get beer!" Beathan shouted. And hippies started lining up for the heady brew. As Beathan poured beer for the hippies, the jug never grew shorter of juice of the barley.

"What did you have me say?" Beathan asked Christ.

"It is a testament to the offerings. All offerings should have flavor. All offerings should please God. All offerings should have salt. Be an offering yourself. Be the salt of the world. We are to add flavor to life!"

It was the great feast of the rapture. It was the homecoming prophesized in the book of Revelations. Jesus returned for his kind. It might not have been the Roman Catholic church Jesus was supposed to return to claim, but these were the kind-heads of the western world. Droves gathered around Christ with respect and attention. Some old wook was nearby roasting green ears of corn as an offering of the first-fruits. The old wook was chanting songs in Aramaic, and the corn multiplied. Everyone feasted. Glastonbury Music Festival was shouting the Lord praises, and he rejoiced with love for those who worshipped him. The world was both primal and electric. The grooves were not only coming from the music, but the fellowship that was taking place in the campground. Folks gathered round to sing praises for Christ. It was the homecoming Jesus had longed for. People who savored life, and found strength and truth in Christ were the target audience. Those who attempted to control him through begrudging, self-righteous obedience never knew him, not like the ones who took the wayward journey of self-discovery, only to wake up hollow relying on the love of Jesus to bring them hope and strength. Still though, there was no salvation without proclamation that Jesus was Lord of all creation. In that moment of jubilee, the mission felt complete. The word was delivered.

Nick and Rafa were still sealed in glass jars, rocking with swell, trying to get out. Music played all afternoon. Now the sun was getting low in the sky, and The Odyssey was taking the stage. The atmosphere had the band intoxicated. Jerry stepped up to the mic once the band was all plugged in.

"Peace be with you!" he addressed the crowd.

"And, also with you!" 135,000 fans shouted in response.

They struck up the rhythm and got down to business. When Allison Krause hit a note in F sharp, the jars that contained Nick and Rafa's watery bodies shattered, and the paddlers flowed out. They heard the music, and rushed to the stage front. There, they saw more people than they ever had, and the peace, love, and joy had reached critical density. It was an atmosphere that was more heavenly and ethereal than any riverbank the kayakers had ever stood upon. Amazing. Nick and Rafa glowed in the environment, but felt mind-boggling confusion.

"Are all these people on acid and ecstasy?" one paddler asked.

They were received with laughter.

"No man! The Lord has returned! Come, join in the love!"

The music played all night in supernatural, psychedelic harmony connecting the crowd with the landscape and atmosphere. Energy flowed through every body of creation, and reverberated a tune that connected each one with its Creator. Individual tastes were satisfied, and the collective passion became dynamic, yet unified through relativity. When it was all over, Jesus slipped away, unseen, to return to his seat at the right hand of God, but God never left his people. The congregation of festivalgoers were grateful for His embrace. How did it happen? Did it matter? Was it important? Everyone wanted to know, and word of Christ's disciples got out. The five of them, Michael Joseph, Beathan, Kyle, Eric, and Todd, were invited backstage to party with The Odyssey.

Eric began telling the story, everything from the time they left Buena Vista.

"This is just the beginning," he started, "but God was with us the whole time. It was incredible…"